Yvonne Coppard was born in London and Devon. She now lives in Cambridgeshire with her husband and two daughters. For many years Yvonne was a teacher in a secondary school, but now she teaches teachers and other adults about child abuse and how to help abused children. Writing books is a lovely way to escape from all that.

In her spare time Yvonne likes to go to the cinema and theatre or out walking on the hills (not in Cambridgeshire, because there aren't any, but she spends a lot of time in Yorkshire!). She also plays badminton and squash; she is pretty hopeless at both of them but reckons that when you know you have no hope of winning, you are at least able to concentrate on having a good time.

By the same author

NOT DRESSED LIKE THAT, YOU DON'T!
GREAT! YOU'VE JUST RUINED
THE REST OF MY LIFE

Everybody else does! Why can't I?

More diaries of a Teenager ....and her Mother

Yvonne Coppard
Illustrated by Ros Asquith

PUFFIN BOOKS

For Reg

PUFFIN BOOKS

Published by the Penguin Group
Penguin Books Ltd, 27 Wrights Lane, London W8 5TZ, England
Penguin Books USA Inc., 375 Hudson Street, New York, New York 10014, USA
Penguin Books Australia Ltd, Ringwood, Victoria, Australia
Penguin Books Canada Ltd, 10 Alcorn Avenue, Toronto, Ontario, Canada M4V 3B2
Penguin Books (NZ) Ltd, 182–190 Wairau Road, Auckland 10, New Zealand

Penguin Books Ltd, Registered Offices: Harmondsworth, Middlesex, England

First published by Piccadilly Press, 1992
Published in Penguin Books 1994
Reissued in Puffin Books 1995
5 7 9 10 8 6 4

I am sick to the tonsils and beyond with GCSEs. I am *supposed* to be doing my Humanities assignment but instead I'm trying to work out what GCSE actually means. It must be one of these:

God's Curse Sent Everywhere

Go Crazy and Senile Easily

Give Common Sense the Elbow.

None of my teachers were ever, ever, young. I know that for a positive fact, because anyone who'd ever been a teenager would realize that the human body can only take so much. I'm young, I'm not bad-looking allowing for the odd zit, and I've got a sense of humour. I ought to be out with friends enjoying life. My friend Catherine has it taped. She uses her mum being in hospital as an excuse to skive. The teachers are what Mum calls 'very understanding' (which is why Catherine's out at the pub now with some bloke, while *I* do the assignment which *she* will no doubt copy tomorrow!). I don't regret asking her to stay while her mum was in hospital, but I'll be relieved when she goes back to her own house. It's been a bit of a strain covering up for her. She has a real talent for sucking up to adults and milking them for every last bit of sympathy, simply to divert attention from what she is really up to. You have to admire her. She has Mum and the teachers all fooled – not sure about Dad. He looks decidedly sceptical sometimes.

My assignment has what the English teacher would call a 'cruel irony' if I were doing Shakespeare – "Give an example of injustice in our society and say how you feel about it. What would you do to put it right?" Easy:

Injustice = making young, healthy people cripple themselves with workloads of boring GCSEs.

Cure

1. Lower the school leaving age to 14.

2. Make GCSEs optional and insist on a sanity test for

those who want to do more than three.

3. Offer compulsory euthanasia to all teachers nominated by thirty or more pupils (a fair safeguard against personality clash, I think). Mr Potter would get a hundred votes dead easy.

5th October

The house is unusually peaceful. Jenny is hard at work on one of her assignments, Jon is tucked up in bed and Mike is working. I am waiting for Catherine to get back from visiting her mother; apparently she'll be allowed home soon, so I suppose Catherine will go back to her own house. Pity; I've enjoyed having her here. I haven't always approved of her as a friend for Jenny, but she's a sweet girl underneath all that tarty make-up and weird hair. I hope everything works out for her now that her mother has got help for her drink problem. Catherine has spent so much time going to see her, attending support groups and what not, and yet she still manages to keep up with her school work. I wish Jenny had her powers of organization.

The children are growing up so fast — I feel quite broody when I see mothers pushing prams . . .

Sadie came round after school, to see if I would come to an Amnesty International meeting with her. Things were a bit strained between us at first – after pinching my boyfriend, she can hardly expect us to be best friends again – but I have missed her since our big bust-up. I can't say I really fancy the idea of this meeting – I don't really know what it's all about, but it doesn't sound like much of a rave. I didn't want to say no, because I do want us to be friends again. So I'll make the best of it.

I was really cut up when David Slater dropped me for Sadie. Funny thing is, I can't for the life of me work out why, now. He's a creep! We only split about three months ago, and he's been out with and dropped two other girls since then. Sadie and I were both taken for a ride. He smiled at me today, all melting marshmallow and gooey charm. I ignored him.

Jenny seems to have made up with her friend Sadie. She has a very forgiving nature; I would find it difficult to trust my best friend if she'd been going out with my boyfriend behind my back. When Sadie came round, a bit shame-faced, I expected Jenny to give her the heave-ho in no uncertain terms. After an initial frost they ended up chatting away nineteen to the dozen. They're going out together at the weekend: very civilized.

It was parents' evening for Jon last night. He loves being a top infant and thinks it's a great responsibility to 'keep an eye on the little ones'. His teacher says he works hard and is always polite and happy. He must have come from a different mould to his big sister. She is not putting in anything like the effort required for the GCSEs. Mike and I are more nervous about the mock exams than she is!

The Amnesty International meeting was not as bad as I thought it would be. They're planning a rally in Trafalgar Square, to protest about political prisoners around the world. If what they said at the meeting is true, then the world is even worse than I thought. How can you torture and starve and beat people just because they don't agree with you? (Mind you, I know some teachers who wouldn't think it a bad idea.) Now I feel bad, because I've made a joke about a serious subject. I always do that with distressing things. Still, I'm going to make up for it. We've been given a list of people to write to – dictators around the world who are holding people without good reason. We were each given a little list of people to write about. I have three. Two of them are in China and one is in Chile. If enough people write, it might make a difference. I wonder if Mum and Dad would let me go on the march? It sounds like a good way to meet a decent upright boy with a heart and a conscience.

11th October

Jenny and Sadie went to a meeting about Amnesty International last night, and came back full of righteous indignation and the wrathful sense of injustice we who are old remember so well. I told Jenny that my generation had protested about all this too. She just said that her generation might actually get something done! Still, I'm glad she has principles. She wants to go on a protest march. Mike and I are reluctant to say yes, but I don't want to deny her the opportunity to stand up for what she believes to be right. We said we'd think about it. We'll see if this is a passing thing, like saving the whales, banning aerosols and the half a dozen other causes she's taken up and dropped.

Jon has chickenpox! He looks AWFUL. Yesterday he was a grouchy little piglet and I was mean to him. Today I feel very guilty about that. He has these incredible blotches all over. Every time you look at him he seems to have a few more. Some of them have little blisters on the top. Mum says they'll all go like that in the end.

I keep wondering what it would be like to have chickenpox when you were fifteen years old. I think I would die of the shame. You'd have to be shut away for weeks, like a leper. All your friends would disown you; it would be terrible. Even being off school for a week or two would be too high a price to pay.

Mum says I had chickenpox when I was a toddler, but I don't remember it. I'm not sure I'm willing to trust her memory. So I'm torn between wanting to help Jon, who's miserable and poorly, and making sure I don't take unnecessary risks. I am putting a bit of 'Dettol' in my bath and washing my hair every day, and trying not to get too close to Jon. I hope it works!

Jon is quite poorly with chickenpox. He has quite a serious dose, and is lying on the sofa like a rag doll, uninterested in anything. He has spots everywhere, including in his mouth and ears and they are very painful. When he gets to the itchy stage it's going to be agony. I feel so sorry for him, and can do nothing to help. It tears me apart watching him suffer.

Jenny is as hard as nails about it. She says sympathetic words, but she treats the poor little boy like a leper. I've told her she can't get it again, but it's made no difference. Frankly, I'm ashamed of her.

Jon is still in an awful state. I have been sitting with him for hours on end while he soaks in baths laced with bicarbonate of soda. Mum sent me to the shop to buy six drums of it – very embarrassing. No-one else I've talked to has heard of bathing in the stuff, so it must be one of Mum's weird Devon remedies from way back. Funny thing is, unlike most of her strange ideas, this one works. Jon doesn't itch half so badly after a bath. I have had to reconcile myself to the risk of me getting it, because Mum has been too busy to look after Jon all the time, and anyway he kept appealing to me to play with him. It just melts my heart when he turns that poor spotty little face towards me (they're even in his mouth – yuk!). Mum, Dad and I take it in turns to keep him smothered with calamine lotion. He's being very brave, and is a bit chirpier today. One of his friends came round for tea – he's a bit spotty too, but not so many as Jon and his are on their way out. It has swept through Jon's class like the plague in olden times. I suggested a chickenpox party but Mum said she thought she might just scream if she had to dab calamine on one more pox!

21st October

Jon is a bit better today. We have splashed our way through gallons of calamine and bicarb baths. He looks like something from a horror movie, but he is beginning to take an interest again, and has had a friend round to play. I am so tired I could sleep for ever – the itching keeps waking him up at night, poor lamb. Mike can't take time off work at the moment, but if Jon's not back to school next week Mike will take over. I am looking forward to being back in the real world rather than this spotty one, and that makes me feel like a bad mother. Blasted chickenpox!

I have spent the whole weekend doing coursework. I wrote three essays and read loads and loads of stuff for Science. (I'm a bit behind. Well, lots behind, actually.) It's half term next week, but the teachers don't see that as a good reason for letting us have some free time. They've loaded on the homework like there'll never be another chance. I've slogged away all weekend in the hope of having some time left to have fun in, but hope is fading fast. My life is so exciting I don't know how I stand it sometimes.

Jon is almost normal looking now, but there are still pale pink blotches everywhere. He's back at school. There are so many of them with varying degrees of spots that he won't get teased about it. It must be really weird to be the teacher, with a whole classful of spotty faces and smudges of pink lotion gazing up at you . . .

I have had a very lazy week, apart from the odd spot of coursework. Cathy is busy with her own social life, and Sadie and I are still getting used to each other again. We've spent quite a bit of time together this holiday, but mostly we watch videos or do homework. It's as if we're both secretly worried we'll say the wrong thing about what's happened in the past, and start a row again.

Sadie wants me to go to a disco with her on Saturday. It sounds a bit draggy – it's at her dad's work. But I had to say I'd go, didn't I? I really want us to get back to being normal friends again. I don't suppose I'll enjoy this do, but it'll be worth it to try and get Sadie back as a friend I can trust.

I've just read my last entry and can't believe I was so casual about the disco – it was mega-brill! Sadie and I had a real laugh together – I've missed her a lot more than I realized. The disco was run by two gorgeous-looking men with all the top music, flashing lights and stuff. It was like a proper night-club but the drinks were cheaper!

Sadie's brother was there with his friend Nick – I've seen him around a couple of times but we've never really talked. Anyway, Nick and I ended up dancing and he was great. He's not bad-looking and he has a lovely personality. He walked me home (Sadie had found herself someone by then, too) and we kissed on the doorstep – not bad at all! We're going to the cinema tomorrow. He left school last year – he's nearly eighteen and so mature, he makes David Slater look like a real wimp.

Went to the latest Jason Priestley with Nick. He bought me chocolates! The film was great, and in the scary bits Nick put his arm around me, which was nice. Afterwards we went to McDonald's and had a burger and a coke. He seems loaded with money – he works for an electronics firm, some apprenticeship or other, but he also works for his dad at weekends sometimes, in the building trade.

Nick is very easy to talk to and I lost all sense of time. I got it in the neck for being late again, of course. Dad went through the usual 'disappointed' – 'thought you had more consideration' routine and I listened to it as patiently as I could. I even managed to look a bit contrite, so he gave up sooner than usual. It was worth it; I had a great evening. Tomorrow Nick's coming round to watch a video with me – Mum and Dad are going out, so once Jon's tucked away in bed we'll have the place to ourselves (Cathy goes home tomorrow, thank God . . .).

November 2nd

What a weekend! The housework seemed to take for ever, perhaps because Jon was trying to help and the people who could have really helped – Jenny and Mike – were too busy enjoying themselves to bother. Catherine went round to clean up her house ready for her mum tomorrow. Mike went fishing all day Saturday, and Jenny has found herself a new boy. His name's Nick, and he's absolutely perfect in every way (just as David Slater was!). They've been out together two nights running and now she's planning to have him round here tomorrow babysitting with her. I asked if that was really a good idea, since she doesn't know him all that well. I was rewarded for my concern with one of those looks designed to wither you to ashes at fifty paces. Mike told her off for being late – again – and she just spun him a line about how sorry she was which he fell for (of course). I've given up trying to reason with her – it's water off a duck's back. I will really miss Catherine, though of course I'm glad her mother's recovering. I have enjoyed having a teenager who actually welcomes an older and wiser opinion.

I long for the days when I could change Jenny's nappy, feed her warm milk and put her to bed. She didn't answer back in those days. They grow up so fast – I always heard people saying that when I was young, but I never realized how true it is. Even Jon is getting too independent to need me – yesterday he said he doesn't want me to take him all the way to school, just to the end of the road. It feels strange – and not nice.

Babysitting with Nick was even better than I hoped it would be. He was great with Jon – they made Lego spacecraft together and then invited me to join them in a game of Monopoly. I began to wonder if the two of them really needed me around, except to ferry coke and crisps from the kitchen. But after Jon went to bed (without too much fuss, for once, because Nick said he could use his Walkman until he fell asleep!) it was *our* time. I showed Nick my records and let him choose the music – he chose all the ones I like best, including great background music for kissing. I'm not going to say too much more, but I learned a thing or two . . .

November 5th

Today was sort of a mixed bag. Potty Potter – the walking Rocky Horror of the Nineties – is in Caring Form Tutor Mode at the moment. This involves chatting to each of his Form individually and giving us the opportunity to chat about individual problems. If you don't *have* any problems, it doesn't worry him at all; he'll simply invent one. In my case, my only problem is him. He gives me the creeps – he's so hairy, for a start, like a mammoth from a prehistoric picture book. There's even hair on the back of his hands! Sadie says we're all hairy, it's just that Potter's shows because it's so dark. We talked about sending him an anonymous note and a bleaching kit to help him out. Sadie is convinced that he fancies Miss Jones (French) and nobody, but NOBODY, could fancy him in his present state. But then, as I said, what has he done to deserve our help?

I digress. Since my only problem is having a time-warp Form Tutor who talks about the Beatles and the Rolling Stones as though they're still alive, and since it would hardly be polite – or intelligent – to point this out,

11

I had to say everything was fine. That gave him the opportunity to invent a problem for me. It's my attitude. I don't care enough about success, I'm not prepared to Strive, to Fulfil my Innermost Potential . . . yawn, yawn. I can't wait to leave school.

The evening was much more fun. I thought it might be wise to store up a few brownie points with the parents, so I made a special point of staying at home for the usual boring family Bonfire Night celebration. Dad always buys a box of fireworks and two packets of sparklers. There are really only three fireworks in this sort of range – rainy ones, bangy ones and shoot-in-the-air ones. But they have names designed to fool you into thinking otherwise. Jon is still young enough to fall for it, and every firework made him squeal with joy, like a young piglet (quite sweet, really). I pretended to be a bit excited too. After I had eaten the compulsory sausages and beans, and roasted a marshmallow over the fire, I was free at last. Thank God for Jon, who is too young and too spoilt to wait until a decent hour for his fireworks. It was all over by eight o'clock, and by half past, Nick and I were at the council display – FANTASTIC!!!! Then we went to the pub. I was legal – only had a coke. But we saw Cathy there, packing away the vodka. Seeing the state her mum's in because of the bottle you'd think it would put her off.

November 5th

We had a real family evening, something that's becoming quite rare now that Jenny is almost grown-up. Bonfire Night has always been a great tradition in our family, and even Jenny couldn't bring herself to break away from it, for all that Mr Wonderful, the new boyfriend, wanted her to go out with him instead. She compromised, and said she would meet him after eight o'clock. For all her image of herself as independent and

12

'hip', she still needs to plug into the family roots now and then. She was almost as excited as Jon about the whole thing.

Mike and I are both feeling a bit down at the moment – nothing specific, just in need of a change, I think. We're both aware that middle age is approaching fast; for me, it's like being stuck in a rut without any real energy to change things. We decided to have a weekend away before the Christmas hoo-ha starts. Mike has a conference in Paris soon, and he can trade in his business class seat for two tourist ones. I'm going to go with him, and we'll stay on for a couple of days after the conference. I haven't had the nerve to tell the children yet – Mike's mother is going to be looking after them. Jenny will hit the roof . . .

I suddenly realized today how near the mocks are – only three weeks away! I've got so much coursework to catch up on before I can even begin to revise for the exam part. I've had to tell Nick I won't be able to see him this weekend. He wasn't too pleased. He doesn't seem to remember what it was like – or perhaps he didn't bother to do any work. But I don't want a heap of trouble falling on me, which is what will happen if I fail everything, so I'm going to be really good and put some effort in. I think Nick understands really.

Work, work, work. If I have to read or write another word I will SCREAM! There has to be more to life than this. Why are we made to go through all this agony? I honestly think I would rather spend my life scrounging from compost heaps than go through all this just to get what Mum and Dad would call a 'decent' job. I phoned Nick to say I would go out with him after all – I was coursework crazy, and couldn't achieve any more. But by then he was already out, with Adam and Jake. I was a bit miffed, but that's not very fair. There's no reason he should miss out just because my life's miserable.

November 16th

A nice, peaceful weekend. I had to work Saturday morning but Casualty was unusually quiet for once and I had a chance to catch up on some paperwork while Mavis manned the reception desk. We have hardly seen the children this weekend – Jon has been playing round at his friend's, 'helping' to build a fish pond, and Jenny is deep in coursework. She seems to have discovered the value of study. It's a bit late in the day, but the mock exams seem to have spurred her on to getting to grips with the various subjects. I admire her staying power. She has even forsaken Nick for the sake of her books. I wish I liked that young man more. He's always polite, seems to treat Jenny well, and dresses smartly, yet there's something about him I don't like. He's just a bit too . . . I don't know. Smarmy? Charming? Or am I just jealous, because all that's over for me now?

Mum and Dad are going to Paris for four whole days next month. What a waste! They're far too old to appreciate the beauties of the most romantic city in the world – Nick and I would make better use of the opportunity. I wish I hadn't told them that, though; Mum went all quiet and said she knew she was getting older but she wasn't over the hill yet. I feel awful now. But I'm being punished, never fear. Grandma Murray is going to come and stay while they're gone! Ever since that awful party last year she has been convinced I need 'firmer guidance' in my 'journey through life'. She gives me this at every possible opportunity. Improving letters with wise sayings copied from books by Patience Strong have arrived on the mat quite regularly, and she could bore for England with her tales of how different life was for her when *she* was fifteen (they didn't have teenagers, then, apparently).

November 18th

We broke the news about Paris today. It didn't go down too well. Jon burst into tears and said it wasn't fair, he wanted to go too. Jenny looked at us as if we were mad and said we were too old for 'dirty weekends away'. I'm getting tired of her attitude to us, as if we were only fit for bath chairs and bedroom slippers.

I don't care. I need this break, and so does Mike. I haven't seen Paris since before Jenny was born, and I've always longed to go back. There's a magic in the air there. It will be wonderful to be just the two of us, sipping chocolat just off the Champs Elysée. I'm going to do all my Christmas shopping there while Mike is at work, and then we'll do the tourist bit together before we come home. I can't wait.

Er, we're taking a little BREAK
You deserve it, Mum. A day in BOGNOR REGIS isn't enough. Why not stay the night?
FOUR days, actually...
In PARIS!
So there
INSEINE! The Lunchpacks of Notre Dame!

Went round to Nick's tonight – his parents are away for the weekend. We got a bit carried away. We didn't actually do anything but it was difficult not to. I like Nick a lot. Just touching makes me feel shivery, and part of me badly wants to do more than we do. He was trying to persuade me that it would be all right; I think he's done it before. But I don't want to take a risk like that without being really sure I'm in love. Nick doesn't see that as being so important. I think it would be better not to be in that situation again!

Sometimes I wish I was more like Cathy, who is quite happy to sleep with anyone she fancies. But when *I* think about going all the way with someone, I can't stop myself wondering how permanent it will be, and what would happen if I got pregnant, or the person I slept with had HIV or something. Mum would say those kind of doubts are a good thing because they protect me from making some terrible mistakes. (I can only imagine what Mum would say, of course. I couldn't really talk to her about it. Parents are only programmed with one response to their children's sex lives – 'Don't!'). I may be a sensible, level-headed person, but the idiots seem to have more fun sometimes.

Jon has come round to the idea of Mike and I being away – he gets spoilt rotten by his gran, and I've promised him something from a French toy shop. I ought to be worried that he is so easily bought off, but I'm just relieved! Jenny is still a bit sulky; she's been very quiet these last couple of days. I'm not sure things are going well with Nick; she asked me to say she wasn't in when he phoned tonight. With her mock exams about to start she needs another dumping like she needs a hole in the head.

Mocks started today – Maths in the morning and Humanities in the afternoon. Trust me to have two exams on the first day. I could have spat when I saw Sadie go home at lunchtime – her next exam isn't for two days. I feel like a bit of old rag. I don't think I did very well – the Maths questions weren't too hard, really, but I just couldn't concentrate. Nick and I had a row last night, because I wouldn't go to a party with him. I knew it would be stupid to have a late night before two exams, and I had revision to do. I suppose I expected he would understand, but he didn't. His friends think I'm a drag, I can tell by the way he shuffles his feet whenever we meet them. They've got working girlfriends, who have pots of money to spend on clothes and make-up and who want to go out and have fun every night. I *want* to do all that, but I just can't. Nick says he knows that, but what he says isn't what he feels. So I felt awful and couldn't revise anyway. This morning he phoned and said he was sorry, and wished me luck. It was a bit late by then!

Mum and Dad are off to Paris tomorrow. Mum's been going round humming and smiling all evening, while packing and writing little notes for Grandma Murray. The old witch will be here when we get back from school. At least she'll keep my nose to the grindstone. Grandpa can't come as he's playing in an indoor bowls tournament. That's really living!

4th December

The bags are packed and the 'plane tickets and passports are lying on the bedside cabinet even as I write. I feel as excited as a schoolgirl. Mike and I should do this sort of thing more often. We've allowed ourselves to become lost in the business of being parents.

Jenny's mock exams started today. I can't say she's made much effort towards them, except at the eleventh hour. I hope she comes through OK. She didn't want to talk about her first two – Maths and Humanities. She just shrugged her shoulders and said they were 'all right'.

I remember when I was taking exams feeling that the whole world had come to a halt; that all there was for me was a desk, sheets of lined paper, a pen and a clock. I felt desolate, as though real life had been taken from me and put on a high shelf where I couldn't reach it. I tried to communicate this to Jenny, but she looked at me as though I was a crazy woman.

6th December (Paris)

This is just as wonderful as I imagined it would be – better, even. The weather is crisp but dry, perfect for walking around. With Mike in the conference I have been wandering round the markets and department stores having a whale of a time. The Christmas shopping is just about done. It's so much easier when you're not trying to fit in work, feeding the family etc. Tonight we celebrated the end of Mike's conference with a quiet dinner in a restaurant overlooking the Seine and then walked around Paris by night. It was lovely. Mike even bought me red roses – the very air here is romantic.

Tomorrow we are going to the ballet (Les Sylphides) after seeing Sacré Coeur and Notre Dame.

8th December

Our last night in Paris. I almost wish we could stay here for ever, although I do miss the children of course. The last few days have been like a dream. It has been so many years since I was here last, and yet it feels just the same. Mike and I have been behaving like a couple of fresh young lovers. There's life in the old dogs yet!

Mum and Dad came back from Paris yesterday. It seems they had a good time. There has been much smiling at each other and holding of hands, and even kisses in the kitchen; it's all a bit pathetic, poor old things. I hope it's a temporary madness and not the onset of mid-life crisis. I'm too stressed to cope with neurotic parents at the moment.

I've had CDT (not bad), Art (OK) and English Lit (yuk – didn't revise) all crammed together over the last couple of days. I went out with Nick to the pub last night. He wanted me to go back to his house but I knew his parents weren't there and I chickened out and said I had to revise. I wish I'd said yes now. There is no excitement in my life whatsoever.

10th December

The children seem to have survived their parents' absence. They obviously missed us very much. Jon's first greeting as we came through the door was 'What did you get me?' and Jenny immediately launched into her 'Life's Unfair' routine. I have pinned a postcard of the Sacré Coeur by night on the kitchen noticeboard, just to remind me I was really there.

Despite the children's best efforts to remind me that I am getting older, nothing will spoil the memories of Paris. It had all the beauty of our honeymoon, all those years ago (but this time we weren't so poor!). Bringing up the children and building a home and career have kept us so busy we forgot how romantic we both are at heart. Just having Mike around to talk to at the end of the day is good enough; the rest is just icing on the cake. I wonder if Jenny will ever understand that? The teenage benchmark for a boy's value seems to be how good he is at kissing and whether he has a car . . .

I haven't written anything for the last few days because there's nothing to write except 'MOCKS'. Are they never going to end? All I have is revision, meals, encouraging pep talks and exams. Nick hasn't phoned me – I told him not to until the exams were over but I still thought he might have. Nothing is happening to me or any of my friends that's worth talking about. The only mild gossip is that Potty Potter was seen pursuing Miss Jones while she was on playground duty yesterday. Big Deal. If there is something going on between them, all I can say is they deserve each other. They are both as weird as can be, they both have the dress sense of a failed clown and they're both dedicating their talents to making the lives of others (e.g. me) as miserable as possible. I must now carry on with my revision . . .

15th December

I did a double shift at work today, and it was chaos. The ambulances were in and out like yo-yos: four road traffic accidents, two broken legs and an attempted suicide. Christmas will not be a happy time for many people. It is easy to get depressed when you work in a Casualty department – particularly when you come home afterwards to a sullen teenager who can talk about nothing except exams. If I have to hear another word about them, I'll scream.

Last exam finished today (Art 2). TERM FINISHES TOMORROW! I feel brilliant (in mood, unfortunately not in brain-power). I don't even care what the results are – at least the things are OVER!

I am going to do my Christmas shopping this weekend and I'm also going to be a wonderful daughter and big sister. Mum and Dad have been really supportive while I've been doing all the exams. Mum's taken an interest in what I've done and how I feel about things, and even Jon has done his bit to help me through. He's been so sweet, drawing me pictures and buying me chocolate bars with his own money. I told him I'd take him out to choose a nice present for Mum and Dad, and I'm going to surprise him by taking him to see the 'Santa Claus' film afterwards. Hopefully, Nick will come too. He thinks Jon is a bit of a pain (which he is, though nothing like as bad as he was with David Slater) but he's very good with him.

19th December

The children came home from school in very jubilant mood today. School has now finished and Christmas can begin. It may be a full six days away, but to Jenny and Jon that's close enough to start celebrating. Mike's getting the tree tomorrow; last year he wasn't even here at Christmas because of work, but this year he's taken leave from tomorrow until the New Year. We go to Mum and Dad's, for a real Devon Christmas, on the day before Christmas Eve. I can hardly wait. I expect Jenny will be a bit of a pain once she's been torn away from her beloved Nick. I almost wish we could leave her behind, but she comes as part of the package for a family Christmas and it wouldn't be the same without her, protests or not.

Another row with Nick – this is getting to be a habit. He doesn't want me to go to the Gramps for Christmas. He's having his eighteenth birthday party on Christmas Eve. Brilliant. What am I supposed to do about it? Mum and Dad would be crushed if I stayed behind (even if they let me, which is doubtful) and so would Jon. Christmas in Devon may be a drag but it would be worse to be separated from them all. Besides, his birthday isn't until the 3rd of January – why on earth does he want to muck up Christmas Eve with a drunken brawl (which is what his party will turn into, knowing his friends)?

I feel really mixed up. On the one hand I fancy Nick like mad – he's mature, he's witty, and he kisses like no-one I've ever met. When I'm with him I could die for him, and it takes all my strength not to do exactly what he wants. But when I'm away from him I seem to remember the bad bits; he's possessive, and not very understanding. Sadie and Cathy say it's simply a physical thing, like those relationships you read about in mags that are just sexual. But ours isn't even that, not yet anyway. So where are we going next? I think being away for Christmas will be a very good thing for me – give me a chance to think.

We arrived home tonight, refreshed and relaxed from a very peaceful Christmas in Devon. Everyone had a wonderful time, even Jenny, who managed to drag herself away from the telephone at surprisingly frequent intervals. On Boxing Day we went to see Mum and Dad's friends, who have a farm. They had an orphaned lamb, only a couple of days old. Jenny and Jon fell in love with it, of course. It was a real old-fashioned country Christmas, just like all the others that stretch back to the time I was born. I am so glad that the children can have them too even though we're not living in the country.

Holding the lamb while it suckled on the bottle made me feel strange, sort of calm and very maternal. It makes me wonder if another child at our age would be such a bad thing. The decision may have been made already. We were not very cautious, Mike and I, while we were in Paris . . . We didn't take precautions the way we normally do.

Christmas in Devon wasn't bad. We ate and drank lots, and I got some great tapes and lots and lots of money. No-one knew what to buy me – they were all very apologetic about it but I was more than pleased to be able to choose my own things (especially considering the relatives I've been blessed with).

Nick came round almost as soon as I was home – he got a car for Christmas! It's a bit of an old banger to look at, but it goes all right. We swished round to Sadie's to offer her and her boyfriend (Mike – a bit dopey but sweet with it) a lift to the pub. I saw the New Year in with cola – honest!

I have only one New Year Resolution. I'm going to be a vegetarian – on weekdays at first, because giving up the Sunday roast would not be a possibility at the moment (unless it's lamb, which I will never eat again). I've overdosed recently because it's just not socially responsible not to lend a hand with everybody's mum's leftover turkey. I've had turkey sarnies at Cathy's, turkey curry at Nick's and turkey à la King at Sadie's. I like to do my duty. Hopefully I'll wean myself off meat and on to proper veggie stuff by next year.

Cathy is staying with us again. Her mum slipped off the wagon in a big way. She went missing two nights ago – having managed to stay sober on New Year's Eve, which Cathy was really chuffed about – and showed up yesterday morning at Casualty, bleeding all over the place. Mum was on duty at reception, and recognized her, which was just as well because Cathy's mum didn't have any idea who she was. Poor Cathy had been staying home alone, not wanting to tell anyone. Dad went over to get her and now she's with us while they sort her mum out – again. She says she doesn't care any more, but you can see she does. How can her mum do this to herself and to her own child? It's horrible. I don't think I'll ever drink again. It destroys everything.

Even Nick's birthday, which should have been great, had the edge taken off by what happened. I told Nick about it when I gave him his present (a 'Heavy Rock' T-shirt). But he just shrugged and said it would work out all right in the end. I thought that was a bit heartless; he didn't really seem very interested. I felt a bit angry, but didn't want to spoil his birthday with a row. When I think about all of us round at Nick's, drinking vodka and cider and acting so cool and witty, it just makes me sick. Cathy's mum probably started off like that. Now Cathy is getting just like her; she puts away vodka and orange like she'll never see drink again. And her boyfriend is really weird; I think he might be doing drugs as well, but Cathy won't talk about him, except to say he's great in bed. Is she joking, or is she really sleeping with him?

Apart from the stuff with Cathy, this Christmas holiday has been really good. Nick and I have only rowed a couple of times, and exams are over.

I forgot I'd decided to be a weekday veggie and have been writing this in between mouthfuls of ham sandwich! I'm going to give up Sunday roast as a penance.

What a terrible couple of days. Yesterday Catherine's mother walked into Casualty in such a state I hardly recognized her. She slumped over the reception desk muttering for help. She was so drunk she had no idea where she was or who she was – someone on the street had guided her to the hospital and left her at the door. There had obviously been a fight, and a broken bottle had been shoved into her neck. An inch or two more and she would have died. There was blood everywhere. Thank God I was there, and knew who she was. We found out that Cathy was at home, and had been for two whole nights, alone, waiting for her mother and worrying herself to death. She's with us now.

Today I went to see Gloria up on the ward. She was barely conscious; I don't know if she was sedated or still suffering the effects of the alcohol. The doctor says her liver is in a terrible state; he's not sure she'll pull through this bender at all. Cathy refused to come with me. She said she no longer had a mother. You can see the hurt oozing from every pore, but she's pretending not to care. What a life. I look at my Jenny and I wonder how a mother could ever allow herself to get into such a state that she could gamble with her own child. But I can't judge her – who knows what I would have done with her situation? It makes me feel very grateful to have such a happy life. I feel ashamed for moaning about the children, and the housework and so on.

We are going to stand by Cathy, because someone has to. But although I am ashamed of myself I cannot help worrying about her influence on Jenny. I know Jenny doesn't drink, but I feel sure Cathy does, and I don't want her to entice Jenny into thinking it's glamorous or clever. I have to hope that Jenny is strong and sensible enough to steer clear.

Back to school – yuk. I was hoping to get some mock exam results, but no. The teachers all lazed about over Christmas, apparently, and it'll be next week at least. Honestly, you'd think that with such long holidays they'd be prepared to make a bit of an effort in special circumstances.

Potty and Jones French have been seen together in a car! Sadie said Jen Walsh saw them at the traffic lights on Saturday. Jonesy saw her and blushed! There must be something in it then. We tried to imagine them kissing, and saying cute things to each other. Sadie reckons they speak French, because that's much more sexy. In form time today she actually asked Potty if he could speak fluent French. He said yes, he could – and then *he* blushed and told her not to look at him in that silly way. Well, it just goes to show how great love is – it can happen to anyone, even hairy monsters and middle-aged women with warts!

Nick took me out for a meal tonight, to commiserate over going back to school. We had spaghetti bolognese – meat again, but I had to eat what Nick ate so our breaths would smell the same. We stayed in the car for a long time when he drove me home, talking and kissing and stuff. The windows got all steamed up. Thing is, I don't really fancy him as much as I did. I'm not sure we're going anywhere. He's funny and generous, but he's not kind or sensitive. He wants me to do whatever he wants, without making allowances for friends or homework or anything. And he wants to go to the pub and laugh about with his mates. I don't like the pub much; the only alcoholic drink I like is cider, and Nick's mates keep trying to persuade me to drink something else. At least Nick doesn't drink much – he sticks to low-alcohol stuff now that he has a car.

Cathy is still with us. Her mum must be very poorly. Cathy still won't go and see her, though. We had a row about it tonight. I said she was heartless, and she said I was a spoilt cow who wouldn't know real life if it reached up and bit me! She said Nick had told his mates that I was frigid, and he wasn't going to keep trying much longer. I wasn't going to write that last bit, because it hurt too much and anyway I didn't really believe it. But it sort of slipped off my pen. It's still at the front of my brain, and I can't think of anything else. Mum heard us yelling – she took me into her room and told ME to be more understanding!

Jan 8th

Cathy and Jenny had a terrible row about something tonight – don't know what was at the bottom of it, but clearly the strain is beginning to show.

I did a pregnancy test today, one of the very early ones. Positive. I can hardly believe it. I told Mike straight away. He went white, and then said these tests were unreliable. I said they were pretty accurate these days, although they do recommend you check the result a couple of days later. I'm going to the doctor's next week, but inside I know it's true. I can just feel it. At first, I thought Mike was shocked and horrified, but then I realized he was worried for me. When we sat down and talked about it we knew we were both thrilled at the idea, even though it would be an enormous disruption.

We are keeping it all very quiet until after next week. Actually, I don't want to spread it about until three months or so has gone past. It will feel safer, more real, then. I have to face the fact that at my age pregnancy is a little bit riskier. I don't want the children to get worried about it all. Considering the fuss Jenny made about us going to Paris, God knows what her reaction will be. The longer I can put off lighting the touchpaper, I will.

A new baby. I hardly dare think about it, in case something goes wrong.

Cathy has gone back home – at last. Her older brother got leave from the army, and they're staying at her house. He's managed to persuade her to visit her mum with him, which is nice. And though I did feel sorry for Cathy, it's nice to be able to have Sadie round for a gossip without having to include her in everything. We haven't seen much of each other lately, what with her Adam and my Nick, and Cathy's problems and all. We spent the whole evening nattering – lots to catch up on. Nick wanted me to go down the pub but I said no. We had a bit of a row. I think we're drifting apart, to be honest. If I had the nerve, I'd finish it. But I don't want to hurt him.

Talking of nerve, the Worm (alias David Slater) cornered me in the corridor today and asked how I was! I ignored him, of course. He said, 'Please, let's be friends.' Like some old line from a movie. I said 'Drop dead.' He looked really crushed. I wonder what he's up to?

And talking of what people are up to . . . Mum is really weird at the moment. She's all sort of dreamy. I spilt coke all over the precious lounge carpet yesterday and she didn't turn a hair – just asked me to please clear it up! And Jon is getting away with murder, and she doesn't even seem to notice. She and Dad are holding hands and stuff again – it was just dying down after that trip to Paris, and now they've started again.

The doctor confirmed it – pregnant! The baby is due on about the 9th of September. She said there was nothing to be concerned about. I'm fit as a fiddle and lots of people have babies late in life these days. I don't even feel as sick as I did with the other two – a bit queasy mid-morning, but nothing to complain about. The doctor's going to keep a special eye on me, and do a few extra tests, but she didn't seem worried. Mike and I went out to celebrate. It's excruciating keeping it from the children and I feel bad about it. But we decided to wait until the tests are all done. Superstition, I suppose. And fear of their reaction.

Since Jenny would smell a rat if we just decided to go out to dinner for no special reason, we told the children Mike was working late and I was going over to a friend's. It was silly, but great fun – when we met at the restaurant we giggled like a couple of kids, looking over our shoulders in case we were followed and concocting a tale of what each of us had done all evening, for when we got home. It was like being teenagers again. This baby (and the trip to Paris, which is what started it all off) has given us a whole new lease of life. I feel wonderful.

I feel awful. I knew Mum was up to something, but I never dreamed she could be so deceitful. I think she must be having an affair! Yesterday she asked me to look after Jon while she went to see Liz. That's her best friend, or as near as parents get to best friends. Dad worked late yesterday and then went to have a drink with the other men in his office. I said I would babysit – Sadie came over and we had a good time once we'd bribed Jon with an extra bedtime story and a promise of a Mars bar tomorrow if he stayed in bed and didn't hassle us.

Round about nine o'clock Liz phoned – wondered if Mum was in! Well, I think I handled it very well under the circumstances. I said no, she's gone to see a friend, could I take a message? She said no, she was seeing Mum next Wednesday anyway, she'd just phoned for a chat.

Sadie could see I was really upset, but I couldn't tell her. Mum lied to me. That was a wicked thing to do – what if there'd been a fire, and I'd had to phone for help? And why would she lie – unless she went off to see a bloke? And Dad slaving away at the office all those extra hours to make money for her. How could she? And what am I going to do about it?

She saw him again today. She worked morning shift at the hospital, but wasn't home when I got in – Jon was playing at a friend's. I asked her where she'd been, and she avoided the question.

It all makes sense now – even the lovey-dovey stuff with Dad. Stands to reason that if she's playing around she'll feel guilty, and also she'd need to make sure he didn't get suspicious. My own mother is prepared to fob her child off on a neighbour so that she can go to some grubby hotel somewhere (I expect it must be a hotel – that's what they all do on TV anyway) for a sordid afternoon. And Dad's all gooey-eyed, thinking she's the cat's whiskers. If only he knew. I can't tell him, though. It'd break his heart.

I went out with Nick tonight – to the pub as usual. I was suddenly sick of it all – and him. When he brought me home I said I felt we should finish it. He wasn't even upset – just said OK, he'd been thinking for a while now that perhaps we weren't all that suited – 'we want different things from our lives,' he said. Oh yes. What he wants is unprintable! So now I've got no boyfriend and a harlot for a mother. Some wonderful life.

Jenny has been very strange in the last few days. She keeps asking where I've been, and what I'm going to do after work etc. It's almost as though she's convinced something is going to happen to me. She looks at me in an odd, hostile way which I think is covering up some deep-rooted fear. Perhaps we're wrong to keep her in the dark about the baby.

I had the first hospital appointment today. It worked out well, because Jon was asked to tea with one of his friends down the road, so I didn't even have to make up an excuse for not picking him up from school. Things have changed a lot since Jon was born. Lots more mod-tech equipment, staff that look like babies themselves (that's the sign of getting old, beyond a doubt!). Everything looks good; they've taken some blood for extra testing because I'm an older mother and I've got to go back to my own doctor in a month, but that's just routine.

Jenny was waiting when I got home, wanting to know where I'd been. She asked if I'd seen Liz again. Jenny is a very curious creature – what's wrong with me seeing a friend? I think things must be going wrong with Nick. They don't spend a lot of time together now. Jenny spends most evenings doing homework, and when they go out at weekends she doesn't come in quite as bright-eyed and bushy-tailed as usual. Things are very tense at home at the moment. I wish she would sort herself out.

Got some results today – finally.
English language, B
Literature, C
French, D
Maths, D
Both the Ds were delivered with 'I told you so' lectures
about not working hard enough. Honestly, they really
believe that sixteen-year-olds have no right to any kind
of life. I work for hours and hours every week. If I can't
get good results, then it must be because I'm just no
good at those subjects, not because I don't make an
effort. Am I supposed to live like a nun, and never have
any fun, or see anybody, or watch TV or bath myself?
I felt so miserable I wolfed down a bacon sandwich
without thinking, and then felt guilty all afternoon.

I'm not telling Mum and Dad about the results. I'm
hoping that the others will be better, and I can slip in the
Ds without them being so noticeable. Besides, with their
marriage going through such a rocky patch because of
Mum's affair I don't want to start off any arguments that
might lead to Things Being Said.

I am really worried about them – what will happen to
Jon and me if they split up? It doesn't seem possible that
Mum could be playing around. She and Dad look so
happy together. Sometimes I don't believe it can be
true, but then why has she been so shifty lately?
Something funny is definitely going on. I wish I knew
what . . .

Feb 7th

We have decided to tell the children about the baby after
Jenny's birthday. I'm not sure how she'll take the news,
and I don't want such a memorable landmark as a
sixteenth birthday to be spoilt by what is likely to be a bit

of a shock. This year, Jenny didn't ask for a party. Last year's was such a disaster I think it put her off parties for life! We're going out for dinner instead, and taking Sadie and Catherine with us as well. I asked Jenny if she wanted Nick to come, but she said they'd broken up. I hadn't even noticed!

I must have been so wrapped up in thinking about the baby that I didn't pay much attention to Jenny. I feel bad about that. Poor little Jon is neglected as well. He looked so mournful when he asked if there was any chance of going to the park after school today that I felt positively wicked. I must make more time for the children.

10th February

Jenny still hasn't had her mock GCSE results – or so she says. She was a bit evasive when I asked her. Perhaps they're awful. In a way I hope they are, because it'll provide a short sharp shock which will hopefully make her pull her socks up in time for the real thing. But she is behaving rather strangely at the moment. She looks at me in such an odd way. And Mike has never had so much loving care and devotion. He's definitely flavour of the month, and I am not. It must be because I refused to buy her yet another pair of jeans last month – but five pairs of identical jeans is enough for any teenager on earth, and I'm disappointed that she chooses to sulk about it. I am trying to jolly her out of it by paying her – and Jon – more attention.

Mum is driving me mad. And Jon. It's like she's extending her guilt trip thing with Dad to us. Suddenly we can't get away from her. She wants to know what I'm doing, where I'm going etc. etc. – not doing the heavy parent thing, just being sort of bright and chatty. Honestly, I think she'd come into the loo with me if she could! Jon keeps trying to creep away to do his Lego, but she searches him out, like one of those modern weapons that locks in on the target and follows it. Once she's found him, she forces him to play Snap and Animal Sixes and all sorts of other games that he is too old for. Last night I found him hiding under the desk in my room, with his Lego helicopter. 'What's the matter with MUM?' he asked, his little face all quivering. 'She won't leave me alone!' Can you be labelled an abused child if your parent insists on forcing kindness and affection on you every minute of the day? Finally I told her Jon and I were going to play together in my room. I did my homework, and he had a blissful hour of peace and quiet to finish his model airport!

12th February

My attempts to spend more time with the children have paid off in ways I didn't anticipate. Last night Jenny actually volunteered to spend some time playing with Jon. They were closeted up in Jenny's room for over an hour, and I didn't hear a single squabble! Just a little effort seems to be drawing us more closely together – a much nicer family atmosphere for a baby . . .

39

Got the last of my results today. I got D in Science and Latin (I had Humanities (C) and Art (B) a couple of days ago). I'm not pretending the results are good. I was a bit shocked. I know I'm not thick, but I have to admit I didn't exactly throw myself into the revision or the coursework. I'm going to have to do much better in the Summer, or I'll end up not being allowed into the Sixth Form and not able to get a job either. I wrote all the results down on a list and gave it to Mum and Dad last night. I thought they would hit the roof, but they just looked sorry for me! Dad said he hoped I'd learned a valuable lesson, and Mum said we all made mistakes and the thing was to make the best of them. Then they both started giggling like a couple of kids. Has Mum told Dad about her fling, then? If so, he's taken it very well – if it were *me* I'd be calling it a bit more than a 'mistake'.

David Slater had the nerve to send me a Valentine card yesterday! It was a sloppy one with hearts and roses all over it, and inside it said, 'I made a mistake – forgive me?' At first I thought it must be from Nick, but when I went to school I saw Slater's stupid grin and knew the truth. He was actually waiting for me, thinking his stupid card would melt my heart. I told him to drop dead. I also told him that if I was the last girl on earth and he was the last boy, it would spell the end for the human race. That got him!

Sadie came round tonight. She and Adam are spending so much time together I hardly see her any more, but her mock results were bad, too, and her parents have said she can only see him at weekends. We intended to study together all evening. In fact, we managed over two hours, but our brains were aching by then so we had a talk instead. It was good. Sadie is in love with Adam; she sort of shines when she talks about him. I don't think I ever shone when I talked about Nick. It was just a physical thing really. I fancied him like mad, but it never went any deeper than a chemical attraction. I'm so glad that we didn't go too far, I thought I was in love with David Slater, but now I can see it was what Mum would call 'puppy love'. If I jumped into bed with every boy I thought I loved, what would be left that was special with the Real love of my life, if and when he comes along?

Now I've got no-one, and that suits me fine, at least until these stinking exams are over. I may as well put my life on hold, and resign myself to the fact that my sixteenth year is going to be a total non-event.

Liz and I went shopping together today after work, and I couldn't resist going into 'Mothercare' to look at prams. The amount of stuff you can buy for babies these days is amazing. I could have bought the whole shop, but Liz managed to restrain me. I came out completely empty-handed, except for a dear little babygro in tartan that was just impossible to resist, and a pair of bootees, and a bonnet.

Tomorrow is Jenny's birthday dinner. It seems impossible to believe she is sixteen. Where did all that time go? How did I get to be old enough to have a grown-up daughter? And now we're starting all over again. I'm *excited and thrilled, but a bit scared too. What if we can't cope?*

I'm also very nervous about Jenny's reaction. Lots of teenagers think their parents give up sex as soon as the necessary family members have arrived. I know Jon will be thrilled — he keeps going on about having a baby brother like his friend Sam. But Jenny might be a bit upset. Ah well, if so, she'll get over it.

My sixteenth birthday! A very civilized affair, not like last year when there was that awful fight. Dad booked a table at this very swish restaurant, and we left Jon at his friend's house for the night. Cathy and Sadie came too. We spent ages on hair and make-up and I must say we looked pretty good. Pity we had to take the parents along; they spoiled the scene a bit, but they were paying!

The waiter was Very Nice – about twenty, with very dark hair and eyes that you could die for. He wished me happy birthday and said I was a 'very sweet sixteen' – not the most original line, but better than nothing.

We had loads of food, but no drink. I had made Cathy promise she wouldn't so much as sniff a glass of wine – she can't stop once she starts. Dad was driving, and Mum has gone off booze for some reason, so it was a very proper, sober do. Nice though. Mum and Dad behaved tolerably well – for once.

My presents were good, too: money and record tokens, a new watch and some tapes, and from Mum and Dad a new Walkman to replace my battered old thing which makes Michael Jackson sound the same as Cliff Richard. All in all, it was a good birthday.

22nd February

We took Jenny, Sadie and Cathy to dinner tonight. I think we should have chosen a more downmarket restaurant – their clothes and make-up looked a bit out of place at The Rose Garden. Still, they seemed to have a good time, so who am I to be snobbish?

I saw the doctor today. All the tests are fine. We are both very relieved and happy. It's hard to believe I'm pregnant at all, I feel so well. Even the bit of morning sickness I did have seems to be getting better. We have decided to tell the children tomorrow. Fingers crossed.

Mum is PREGNANT! I can hardly believe it. That is the most DISGUSTING thing EVER! Jon and I are shocked to the core. How could they, at their age? It's hardly a responsible way to behave. They should be looking forward to grandchildren, not planning more of their own. I just can't believe it. Mum just came right out with it at dinner. 'I've got some wonderful news,' she said. 'We're going to have a new baby – in September.'

September! I might be out at work by then – at the very least I'll be in the Sixth Form. How am I supposed to face people, when this gets out? I'll be the laughing stock! At least I know what the big secret has been all these weeks – Mum took one of those early pregnancy tests, and she's known for ages but not thought to share it with Jon and me. She said she wanted to make certain all the tests were okay. I wish now that she HAD been having an affair – at least it would be private. You can hardly keep a new baby a secret.

I am about as upset as I've ever been with Mum and Dad. I'm upset with myself, too. I was so shocked I said some horrid things, things I'm too ashamed even to write down. Mum was crying and Dad went all white by the time I stomped out of the room. I've cried, too. My eyes are closing up with it. And Jon came into my room and we cried some more. Then Jon said he hoped it was a boy, because then at least he could play with it. I went downstairs to say sorry. Mum smiled and said it was all right, but I could see she was really shaken up. And I couldn't say I didn't mean what I said. That would be so easy to see through.

Poor little baby – they'll be in bath chairs by the time it's my age, and it's not the baby's fault. We'll have to make the best of it. Somehow, I'll have to live down the shame. I know Cathy and Sadie will stand by me. It's at times like this you find out who your real friends are.

Well, whether this baby is a boy or girl, I can be sure of one thing – there'll be cold cheer at its birth in this house. We told the children tonight. Jon immediately burst into tears and said we were telling lies and anyway he didn't want a baby. That was bad enough, but Jenny had a real field day. Her first question was whose baby was it? I thought Mike was going to hit her. But she seemed to me to be asking a genuine question. She must think Mike is too old to father a child. After the initial bomb drop she followed up with sniper fire. Did I realize there was a population explosion? It was selfish for people of our age to grab more than our fair share, not to mention disgusting. How was this baby going to cope when it went to school and all the other mothers were twenty years younger? That one hit the bullseye – it's been on my mind a lot too.

Jenny and Jon stormed upstairs together. Later Jenny came down to say sorry, but we both knew she meant every word. Mike says it's a typical teenage reaction and to take no notice. Jon must have just been shocked, because when I put him to bed he was chattering about what he was going to teach the baby, and how he would let it share some of his toys (as long as it's a boy, and there seems no doubt in his mind about that). Mike is furious with Jenny and wants to give her a good talking-to, but I stopped him. I think she feels bad enough. As for me, I'm too crushed to be angry. The birth of a baby should be such a joyful thing. This one seems to be destined to cause sorrow.

Things have been awful at home since I last wrote in this diary. I have tried to make it up to Mum, but every time I look at her I feel angry. How could she do this? And she looks at me as if she is waiting for me to attack her again, which makes me feel guilty, which makes me angry with her – and so on. Dad is more normal; he's sort of pretending nothing happened between Mum and me. Jon is absolutely nauseating. He's told all his friends about the baby, and he's really excited. Mum said he could help choose the name, and so far he's chosen Asterix, Todd or Jonathan! He sees no reason why there can't be two Jons in the family. Big Jon and Little Jon. I think William would be nice for a boy, and perhaps Elizabeth for a girl, then she could be called Lizzie, Libby, Lisbet, Beth – loads of things. Not that anyone has asked me what I think. I don't blame them, after what I said about the baby. But since Mum is clearly going to go ahead and have it, I am prepared to make the best of it.

I told Cathy and Sadie about the baby. Sadie thought it was great, and couldn't see why I was so shocked. She wished her parents were still capable of that sort of thing, she said. I suppose she has a point. Mum and Dad aren't as lifeless as some parents I know. Cathy felt very sorry for me. She said babies are a real pain in the neck. Her mum has had at least two abortions, Cathy said. That shocked me; she talked about the whole thing as if it was just one way of dealing with an inconvenience. I did wish, straight after I knew, that Mum would miscarry or have an abortion, but I feel really ashamed of that now. I couldn't do it, and would hate to think that Mum could.

Talking to Cathy and Sadie made me realize that having a baby in the family might not be such a bad thing. Now I have to figure out a way of convincing Mum that I'm not sending out evil vibes.

Sadie is in hospital. She's very ill. She has osteomyelitis, a sort of bone disease. It's very rare for a girl her age to have it, apparently. At first, her parents thought she was going down with the 'flu, but her GP has worked in countries where osteomyelitis is a bit more common, and he whipped her into hospital. Mum says it's an infection of the bone, and it might have started up after Sadie fell off her bike a couple of weeks ago. That bit is scary, because it wasn't even a serious wound. She limped a bit for a couple of days, and then said it was OK. Now she's in hospital, and has had an operation on her leg. She's going to be in plaster for a while, and then she'll have to wear a sort of caliper for a while after that. She might need more operations; they don't know yet. They won't even let me visit, not for at least three days the hospital said. Her mum has taken in flowers and a card from us all. I am so upset I can hardly think straight. What if she had died? And the last conversation I had with her, I was so busy whingeing on about Mum and the baby that I hardly noticed she wasn't well.

While we were having dinner tonight I just started crying. I couldn't help it; I suddenly pictured Sadie lying there in pain, all alone, and started sobbing. Mum was great. She just gave me a big hug and said Sadie would be all right, and she would need a friend very badly when she came out of hospital. She won't be going out much with her leg in plaster. If only she's all right, I'll spend every spare minute keeping her company, I don't care. I've written her another note saying I'm going to rig up a home disco kit for wheelchair users, so we don't have to leave home to have a good time. I hope it cheers her up.

Jenny's best friend, Sadie, has developed myelitis. They operated on her last night. It's a serious thing for a girl of her age, and very rare in the Western world, according to the Casualty Consultant I spoke to at work today. He said Sadie'll be fine once they've cleaned up the abscesses on the bone (the operation) and pumped her with antibiotics but recovery can be a bit slow. We'll have to see. Jenny is very upset; she can't stop crying. I've told her to stay at home tomorrow if she feels unable to cope at school, but I can't do much to help her. I wish we hadn't been at loggerheads these past few days. Since I told her about the baby things have been strained, to say the least. Now I want to reach out to her, but there's such a distance between us I'm not sure she'll let me.

Things like this surely help you put life into perspective. I have found it difficult to forgive Jenny for what she said to me, but what if it was her lying in hospital tonight? Life is too short to carry grudges. Besides, Jenny is basically a very kind-hearted and loving person and although I do get frustrated with her narrow-minded teenage perspective on the world sometimes, I love her very much and I'm quite proud of her, too.

I hope we can both come to terms with the differences that the baby will make to us both, and get back to where our relationship was – sort of armed neutrality with an occasional outbreak of peace and affection!

I saw Sadie. She was as white as a sheet, but she managed to smile at me and chat a bit. Her whole leg is in plaster. She says it's not very comfortable, but it's only while the bone knits together and grows again. She doesn't know how long that will take.

I promised Sadie I would go in tomorrow and take work from school. She's worried about losing so much time before her exams. I tried to comfort her – if she fails, it'll only mean we'll be doing the retakes together (after my mock results I'm not too hopeful of getting through first time!).

In the Red Cross shop at the hospital I saw these gorgeous little bootees. They were a real work of art, and made me wish I still had a doll to play with! Since they were reduced to half-price as well as being very pretty, I bought them for the baby. When I gave them to Mum she started crying. It was dead embarrassing. It must be all the hormones.

Jenny finally seems to be coming round to the baby. Today she went to see Sadie at the hospital, and came back with a pair of bootees she had bought for the baby. It was a symbolic gesture I think, both a request for forgiveness and an expression of woman-to-woman solidarity. I feel very happy with everything now. This baby will be welcomed after all.

I have signed up for ante-natal classes, as it was so long ago since we had Jon that I think I've forgotten everything! Mike is a bit reluctant to come, but by the time the first class starts I'll have coaxed him round. We are both a bit embarrassed about being oldies, but my doctor says half the people on the course will be our age – and it'll only be their first baby! Times are a-changing.

I looked through one of Mum's books about babies and childbirth, so that I know what I'm in for. Mum's been lucky not to get morning sickness, but apparently she'll be luckier still to escape other effects later on: swollen ankles, puffy face, brown blotches on her skin, backache, babies lodging themselves in odd places, high blood pressure – the things that can go wrong are amazing. She'd better take it especially easy, being what the book calls 'a mature mother'.

I went shopping with Mum on Saturday. I'm not doing that again until after the baby's born. I can look at cute baby dresses, pushchairs, blankets and baby alarms for just about five minutes without feeling like my skull is having a hole bored through it, but Mum could have browsed among the nappies all day. I only survived by dragging her off to the café for frequent infusions of coke (me) and milkshake (her). I am past being embarrassed by the sight of my mother downing a milkshake in public. I have developed a great line in sheepish grins when I meet anyone I know. When Mum's stomach gets big I'll have to avoid being seen with her in public, but until then someone has to keep her in check, or this baby will have a pram for every day of the week, an exhausted and aging big sister and bankrupt parents!

Sadie came out of hospital yesterday. She won't be back at school for ages, because she can't lug her plaster around and in the wheelchair she can't get up the stairs at school. A home tutor is going to help her keep up. I said I'd go round every day in the Easter holidays and study with her, too. They start next week – can't wait! Just as well I have no love life – I'll be able to help Sadie and catch up with all my GCSE stuff as well!

Poor Sadie is feeling very down at the moment. Mr Marvellous (Adam) didn't come to see her in hospital very much. She doesn't think he went out with anyone else, but she was upset that he didn't seem to care. I thought that was a bit harsh – he might just hate hospitals – but Sadie has decided to see a bit less of him while she's off school. Although it's Sadie that is doing the dumping (actually I suppose it's a half-dump, since he still comes around her house a bit) she is very sad about it. On top of feeling poorly and being almost completely immobile, it must seem awful. She will need lots of support over the next few weeks.

March 19th

Everything is going brilliantly well for us all at the moment. Mike has been promoted to European Manager – it will mean more trips abroad, possibly even going to live there at some stage in the future, but it's a wonderful opportunity. It's also more money – once we'd promised we wouldn't be moving until she'd finished school, that was what prompted congratulations from Jenny!

People at work are being very sweet about the baby, and there's a bit of fussing about getting me to sit down and take regular snacks etc. Jenny, too, is becoming a bit of a mother hen. We went shopping together a few days ago and she kept insisting that I stop, sit down and have a drink after almost every shop! It was so sweet to see her concern for me and the baby.

Jon is disappointed that I'm not blowing up like a balloon. We bought him a copy of 'How Babies are Made' and he has developed an embarrassing habit of opening it up to a gruesome-looking diagram of a woman with a see-through tum and gathering his little friends round to compare the picture with me! I think that book might become inexplicably mislaid soon.

I made it! I have been a vegetarian for three weeks without eating a single bite of meat. My only hiccup was a bag of smoky bacon crisps, which I genuinely didn't realize I was eating until it was too late. I am doing my bit to save animals from slaughter, and I am a living testimonial to the benefits non-meat diets can bring. Dad – a steak and chips man – is positively weedy and pasty-looking beside me. Mum is beginning to eat less meat, and Jon announced yesterday that he wants to be vegetarian too. Then he found out that meant no burgers and no sausages, and changed his mind. Children are so unreliable.

David Slater telephoned last night. I thought he'd finally got the message that I wasn't interested, but he was asking me to a party next Saturday. 'Just good friends,' he said. I told him I was going over to Sadie's, because she's still in plaster for another week. He seemed quite concerned about Sadie, too. Perhaps he likes to keep in touch with all the girls he's dumped, just in case he gets desperate for a date sometime. I put this to him and there was a long silence. Then he said, 'You really hate me, don't you?' That made me feel funny. I said no, I didn't hate him, but I just wasn't prepared to be messed about. He said he'd been immature the first time we went out. Now he realized he had handled it all wrong, and wanted to be friends. I said OK, friends, and I'd think about seeing him again.

We did have some good times, David and me. All in all, it was better than with Nick, because there wasn't the same pressure. But I don't know about going out with him again – I'll see what Sadie thinks.

STOP PRESS! The Fourth Form school trip to France is being organized by Potter! That cannot be a coincidence, especially as he blushed when he told us he was going to be away in France and caught Jen and me looking knowingly at him. Jen says he should just come clean and tell us what the state of play with him and Jonesy is. We could probably give him some good advice on how to proceed. The poor man clearly needs some. He must be at least forty, and he hasn't caught any unsuspecting female yet. Jonesy (who is not truly female, if you know what I mean – she's rather plain and warty) is his best chance.

I await news of the French trip with interest. After all, look what happened when Mum and Dad went to France together . . .

I've got a babysitting job for one of Mum's friends. It's only round the corner, and they're going to need me at least once a week, so I'll have enough money to go out and enjoy myself a bit more often – once Sadie's better.

The Easter holiday seems to have gone by without me really noticing, apart from the eggs. I must admit I spent two or three days stuffing myself with chocs, but otherwise it could have been any old weekend. Sadie says vegetarians shouldn't eat chocolate because it contains animal fats. But I think that's asking too much of anybody, and I'm sure the animal population would understand, and make an exception for choccy. It is such a consolation to the terminally dull life.

My love life is non-existent, Cathy's doing enough for both of us and is rarely around, and so I spend most of my time with Sadie. We sit around and talk – although we're running out of things to say – and we watch videos and do homework. What a way to spend Easter! On Bank Holiday Monday, the rest of the family went out to a National Trust place. I even fancied the idea of going along with them, my life had become so boring! But Sadie wouldn't come, even though Dad could easily fit her and the chair into the car. Her own mum and dad don't seem to know what to do. They just give in to her all the time, and they've let her become a recluse, locked up in that house waiting for life to pass by. It can't be right. Anyway, I felt bad about her being alone all day so I stayed home too. We ate our Easter eggs and played Monopoly and watched telly. I am so sick of telly now I don't think I'll ever watch it again once Sadie is better. My head feels like a square stuffed with cotton wool.

Actually Sadie is quite difficult to be with these days. She moans all the time about her leg, and how bored she is. I'm sure I'd moan too if it was me, but it's not easy having to sit and take it night after night. The plaster is coming off soon; she'll still be in a wheelchair for a while because the bone will be weak, but I could push her round the shops and stuff. She won't even consider the idea. She says people will stare at her, and she'll get wedged in doorways and left outside anywhere that has stairs. It seems she's been thinking about all the places we usually go, and none of them are suitable for wheelchairs. That's disgraceful. I wish there was something we could do.

Meanwhile, I am more or less a prisoner. I'm even looking forward to going back to school, that's how bad it's got! I said I'd be her friend and I will, but I hope she gets better soon. When will I be free? I didn't even go out with David Slater to the party because she was upset about it. The only outside life I have at the moment is being lived through Cathy, who tells me exactly what she's been up to, and with whom. I think I've taken the place of her mother, who is still struggling to stay sober (and doing quite well at the moment, which may be why Cathy wants to keep her in the dark about what she's up to!). I tried to talk to Cathy tonight about all the risks she is running, sleeping around like she does. She said she was careful, and I didn't have the guts to ask anything more.

7th April

I am at that awful pregnancy stage of looking too plump but not pregnant. Nothing fits, but maternity dresses look daft. I feel like a proper frump. Jenny offered to lend me some of her vast T-shirts and jumpers last night. They're massive on her, which is how she likes them. They only just fitted me. She and Jon shrieked with laughter, which did my ego no good at all.

Jenny is working very hard on her schoolwork. It is a sad fact that Sadie's illness has been a blessing in disguise for Jenny. She has to stay in with Sadie, and I

*admire the selfless way she sticks by her friend, giving up
her own social life without a murmur of complaint. Jenny
has worked so hard over the school holidays to catch up
all the coursework she needed, and she's really knuck-
ling down at last. I think she's even beginning to enjoy
the quiet life.*

9th April

My first proper babysitting evening at our neighbours',
the Smiths. I've been round a couple of times to get to
know the kids, but this was the first time alone with them.
It went quite well. The older one, Jessica, is nine and she
just sits and watches TV most of the time. Then there's
Micky, who's just five, and he's a bit of a handful. He
made me read three bedtime stories (Jessica told me
afterwards he's only allowed one). Before he would
even consider going to sleep, he made me look under
the bed for dragons, get two drinks of water, search
everywhere for his toy snake – what kind of child goes to
bed with a toy snake, I ask you? He makes Jon look like
a little angel. But when he finally did get to sleep – about
nine o'clock – he looked so cute.

Jessica went to bed at half past eight like a little lamb.
By the time their parents got home at ten-thirty, I had
even managed to tidy up the toys and games they had
sprawled everywhere and did some revision. Not a bad
evening's work – and I was well-paid, too!

When I got home Mum said David Slater had called
again. Also a boy called Jamie. The only Jamie I know is
one in Form 10H, the year below me, and I have no idea
why he should be phoning. So who is this mystery man,
and what does he want? (It sounds like the stuff you find
on a book cover.)

Mystery solved – it was the Jamie from the year below me. He asked me out today, while we were standing in the lunch queue. What's more, before I could tell him no, I saw David Slater out of the corner of my eye and knew he was going to be asking me out again too. Suddenly I was saying yes, I'd love to go bowling with Jamie on Saturday.

My brain must have gone on leave without me. I mean, Jamie's a nice enough boy, but he's both younger and about two inches shorter than I am! I've talked to him occasionally in the dinner queue, and that's all. It's never, ever crossed my mind to look on him as a potential boyfriend. It did get David off my back, but what am I going to do on Saturday?

Jamie is lovely! How could I have missed him all these years? At school, he's such a tough guy – in the football team, boxing a bit at weekends, always in trouble for not doing homework etc. But when you get him on his own he's easy to talk to and a good listener. His bowling is almost as bad as mine, and we laughed like toddlers over all sorts of silly things. He has a little sister the same age as Jon, and we compared notes. You can see he thinks she's great, even though he moans about her a bit. He has two brothers (aged eleven and three) *and* two sisters (nine and six). I told him about Mum and the baby, and he said he'd be able to give me lots of advice.

Jamie's nothing like the macho man he always pretends to be at school. And though he is younger than me, he seems so mature. The evening just flew past. When he took me home on the bus he put his arm round me, and when we got to the front gate he kissed me. That was all – not like Nick, who had octopus tendencies. It was a great kiss, too. I think he must have had more practice than me, for all his tender years!

We're taking Jon and Meggie (his sister, Megan) to the park after school tomorrow. Then I'll have to go on to Sadie's. Jamie only lives two doors away from Adam, and said it was a shame Sadie didn't want Adam, because he was gutted when she told him not to come round. When I said it was more the other way round, that Adam hadn't visited in hospital he grinned like mad and said that was OK, then, it would all sort itself out. He's going to talk to Adam, and I'm going to talk to Sadie. There's been a breakdown in communication. Adam couldn't go to the hospital because he was so worried about Sadie he thought he'd get embarrassing and cry or something! Then she seemed to cool off, so he thought he'd better, too. What a tangle of minefields love can be, eh?

Jenny seems to be rejoining the world of romance. She went bowling tonight with a very nice-looking boy called Jamie. Not Jenny's usual type – maybe she felt sorry for him. He's a bit smaller than she is, for a start. She likes tall men. He's also very clumsy; he dropped his coat on the floor, then his door key, and finally fell over the doormat on the way out. He has the look about him of a faithful terrier, and he's obviously very keen on Jenny. You can tell by the sort of eager way he looks at her. I hope she's not too hard on him. I can't imagine how this date occurred. Jenny must have been thinking about something else when she said she'd go out with him. Maybe she's stir-crazy after all those nights of vigil at Sadie's bedside. Her verdict when she came home was that Jamie was 'OK, I suppose'. I don't give much for his chances of a long-term relationship!

Jenny actually volunteered to take Jon to the park this afternoon. I could have fainted with the surprise! It seems her new young man, Jamie, is the oldest of five children and very mature and responsible. He came round with his little sister, Megan. She goes to the same school as Jon, and they seemed to be quite good friends. So off they went, a happy little family group. I can't believe Jenny could have chosen such a nice boy to go out with. He hardly fits the teenage rebel life she tries so hard to create. I bet he buys his mother flowers on her birthday!

I have got used to the idea of being pregnant now. I used to think about it all the time, but now I've settled into a more routine sort of contentment. I don't feel anxious about my age any more; the baby will have known nothing different, and it's not such a big thing these days. It'll be wonderful.

I dropped by at Sadie's after school, as usual. She's going around on crutches now for short spells but it will be at least another two weeks before she can get back to school. She looked so sad and pale while I was telling her all the school gossip. (With typical timing, Adam has been off school for over a week with flu, so Jamie hasn't even had a chance to tell him about Sadie!) Even the latest stage in the Jones-Potter romance failed to cheer her up. They had a row almost in front of everybody yesterday. They were in the French room together when our class arrived for the lesson. Things were obviously getting a bit heated, but when he saw us at the classroom door, all agog, Potty Potter slammed it shut! A couple of minutes later, Jonesy opened it, Potter stalked out looking like a black cloud about to burst, and Jonesy was mean all lesson. Her eyes looked a bit red, too. Could this be the end of the Romance of the Century? Cathy and I talked about writing a little love note for each of them pretending to come from the other. But we need Sadie for that kind of thing. She has a knack of producing very convincing romantic stuff – it's all the Mills and Boon romances her mum has stacked around the place, I suppose. It sort of rubs off. So we decided we would have to leave the silly pair to sort themselves out.

Anyway, having failed to cheer Sadie with tales from school or Jon's latest little cutenesses I was at a bit of a loss. I was just about to leave when she suddenly burst into tears – a real flood – and said she felt as if her life was over! She was being serious, too. I felt so helpless. She feels trapped and ill and ugly all the time. She's scared to go out but hates staying home. Her mum and dad keep fussing over her and driving her mad and she can't see the future being any better. I gave her a big hug and let her pour it all out, but I didn't know what else to do. I'm so worried about her. It's no use talking to her parents. They're worried enough already.

April 21st

Jenny was going round the house like a shadow all day. I asked her what was wrong but she just shrugged. Then after lunch I asked her when she was going to Sadie's this weekend (I had bought a little gift to cheer her up) and Jenny was a bit evasive. She got very snappy when I persisted. I was only trying to take an interest. The poor child must be fed up to the back teeth with being stuck in the house all the time. Jenny says she won't go out because people will stare and she can't get the wheelchair in and out of buildings etc. I must admit I had never really thought about this. At the hospital, we take all the ramps and other facilities for granted, but out in town and so on it must be very hard to get about for anyone with a disability. I said someone ought to do something. Suddenly Jenny shouted 'Yes, they should!' and grabbed her coat. She galloped off to Sadie's with the look of someone on a mission. I do hope she's not going to do anything embarrassing that involves being brought home by someone official!

I have not been able to get Sadie off my mind. It's awful to see your best friend in such pain. I keep thinking of all the times I've been mean to her. When she was going out with David Slater I would have given anything to see her suffer like this, and now I feel guilty, as if I've somehow wished it on her.

Anyway, Mum was rabbiting on about how people should do something about people in Sadie's situation when it came to me – the Grand Plan. I grabbed a couple of notepads and charged round to Sadie's with my idea. I told her it was up to us to channel her suffering into something that would benefit mankind. It was quite a magnificent speech, actually, and made me wonder if I should take up politics. I don't think my election speeches would be half as boring as the ones given by the sleek, groomed people in boring suits who run the country at the moment. But I digress. I managed to persuade Sadie to come out with me to a few places like the library, a department store and a public loo. Instead of trying to disappear into the background we made a big thing out of Sadie being in a wheelchair. If she couldn't get into a place (the public loo was worst – fifteen steps! It's bad enough having to sit in a wheelchair without being forced to develop an iron bladder!) we both got out our notebooks with a flourish and had a loud conversation about the lack of facilities for the disabled, making notes as we went. The manager of 'Smith and Henson' (the chair couldn't get between the racks of clothes without knocking half the stuff over) got quite het up, and even said he would look into the problem 'with the utmost sincerity and urgency'. Talk about crawlers. He kept smiling nervously over his shoulder. I'm sure he thought there was a hidden camera somewhere. After that we pretended to each other that we were on a special assignment for a consumer programme, like 'That's Life'. Sadie was giggling again by the time we got to McDonald's for tea (my treat, thanks to the babysitting job). Then came the best bit. I had arranged to meet Jamie there – and he brought Adam with him. I was as surprised as Sadie, and she looked flabbergasted. Poor old Adam was still pale and weedy looking from being ill, but when Jamie and I tactfully left them alone they were clasped together like babes in the wood. It was dead romantic. I have a feeling I'll have a bit more free time now.

I should have known it would be too good to last. Sadie is a lot better, and her boyfriend has apparently returned now that she can provide good company again. Sadie seems to have forgiven him for deserting her when she most needed him; the young could teach we older ones a thing or two about forgiveness, maybe. Now Jenny is reverting to her old ways. She's out with Jamie at every possible opportunity and the old homework rows have started again. She says that she and Jamie study together, but that's not what they called it in my day!

I am leaving all the fighting to Mike as far as possible, maintaining a calm and relaxed lifestyle so as not to give the baby bad vibes. I want it to be born into smiles and caresses, not angry thoughts and recriminations. I have developed the art of positive thinking, and I have never looked or felt better.

Poor old Mum looks quite haggard these days. She looks awfully fat, considering there's nearly five months to go. I don't suppose her figure will go back afterwards. I'm reading a couple of books Sadie got me from the library, one on middle-age crisis and one on post-natal depression. I feel it's as well to be prepared!

Bank Holiday weekend was celebrated in great style. I studied all day, every day. My first exam is in four weeks' time. I can hardly believe it. Jamie is insisting that we don't see each other more than twice a week until the exams are over, so that I can study. Honestly, it's like being with Grandad sometimes! But he really cares about me doing well, and he's very sweet. It's not love, but we enjoy being together. There's no pressure to do more than kiss and hold hands and stuff like that.

Cathy is staying with us again. Her mum went on another bender. Cathy is talking about leaving school and getting a job. I think she thinks her mum may not be around to support her through the Sixth Form. I can understand why Cathy has to escape from her rotten life so often, though I think she's stupid to drink so much and sleep around the way she does. At least at the moment things are a bit steadier in that department. She's been going out with this one man, Ted, for over a month now. He's twenty-seven, and he's married, but she doesn't seem to care. She gets very scornful about Jamie – my "Little boy" she calls him.

I have tried very hard to make allowances for Cathy and I accept she's having a terrible time, but the strain of not fighting back got to me in the end. What with all the pressure of exams coming up and a new baby on the way it's like walking on eggshells in this house, holding your breath in case you put a foot wrong and crush someone. Inside I have been getting more and more angry at the way Cathy treats my home and family as her own. She takes Mum for granted. All right, I suppose I do, too, but that's normal when it's your *own* mother.

Last night Cathy made a joke about Ted telling some story to his wife about where he was when actually he was with her. Suddenly I snapped and we had a blazing row. I called her a drunken slut and a home wrecker. It was over the top, I know, and she slapped my face. I don't say I didn't deserve that – who am I to know what she's going through? but she ought to make an effort while she's staying with us. Poor Mum gets so upset if she thinks we're quarrelling. And she usually blames me, since poor little Cathy has been so Cruelly Treated by Life that we all ought to make up to her for it. Yuk! The only way Cathy and I can get along right now is to not speak.

May 5th

Gloria is back in the clinic and Catherine is back with us. It is hard to think positive thoughts and feed my baby soothing messages with the tension that's going on between Cathy and Jenny at the moment. Last night they had a real humdinger of a fight. They wouldn't say what it was about. As the exams get closer I suppose it will all blow up again. Basically, they are very different people. Cathy is as tough as old boots, and I have the sneaky feeling that she's very good at manipulating people. I think Mike and I have been strung along by the sweet innocent act, but I have this feeling that Cathy is far more devious than she appears to be. Why doesn't she want us to meet her boyfriend? She says he's nothing special and she doesn't want to encourage him, so why do they spend over an hour in his car when they come back from a date? And how come he has one of those very flashy cars if he's 'about eighteen' as she so vaguely puts it? I smell several rats. I hope she's not with us too long; I can't take too much high drama at the moment!

Jenny appears to be working very hard for her exams. I hope it's not all an act. At least she has done one sensible thing; she has arranged to see Jamie only twice a week until the exams are over.

Jamie and I went out rollerskating tonight. If I had to look at another textbook I would have screamed. I just had to get away. Jamie listened to all my grumbles about the pressure, the revision etc. etc. and then just smiled and said, 'Soon it'll all be over.' I told him he was very understanding, and he said he was just hoping for the same kind of treatment when it was his turn! It's funny, I never think about Jamie being younger than me. We feel like an old married couple. There's no real passion, and even if I wanted to swap bed tales with Cathy I wouldn't be able to, and yet it doesn't matter. Perhaps we are destined to grow old together, safe and comfortable with our bedsocks and old age pensions rather than passing through the sowing of wild oats and the highs and lows of teen romance. Would that be so bad? I certainly wouldn't want Cathy's life. She and Ted are at it almost every spare moment, if she's to be believed. She says his wife knows about her, and they're going to split up soon. Then she and Ted will get a flat together. But why hasn't he left his wife *now* if he's so potty about Cathy? She has no answer to that. I think she's being taken for a ride.

Jamie came round for Jenny tonight. They look very good together, I must say. They sort of mould into one, somehow. I have awful worries about how close they are. I try to be very modern about these things, but I'm worried to death that she might be committing herself too soon. I have tried to broach the subject of contraception without being obvious, but I haven't had much success. We talk in broad general terms but she never asks me any specific questions or shows any sign that she wants to confide. I have had to resort to leaving

suitable literature around and hoping she will read it.
(This backfired yesterday, when Jon waved a magazine
under my nose and asked me what 'safe sex' was. I told
him I didn't know, and asked if he wanted a cheese
sandwich!)

May 15th

Mum is clearly having second thoughts about the baby.
She hasn't said anything specifically, but she's reading
up on methods of contraception. I don't think she knows
as much as she should (well, that's obvious isn't it, or she
wouldn't have got pregnant at her time of life). She has
tried hard to steer me into conversations about contraceptives on the pretext of 'helping' my education. But I
think she's just trying to get advice for the future without
admitting ignorance. It is the responsibility of every
caring teenager to give his or her parents good quality
sex education. But I'm not exactly an expert, am I? The
closest I came was with Nick, and Jamie is hardly likely
to provide me with the opportunity to become an
expert. I'm not too worried, though. At least she's
buying the right magazines. I'll just be on hand if she has
questions.

My exam revision is going really well. I am actually ahead of the revision timetable Potty Potter set up for us (in between his love trysts with Miss Jones), so I celebrated with a real night out on the town. Jamie was away for the weekend, so Sadie and Adam and I went to her dad's social club again. Sadie is on crutches now, and getting around well. She and Adam are made for each other, you can tell just by looking at them. They sort of shine when they look at each other, it's really sweet. Sadie's mum and dad like Adam too.

Well, I was just drinking a coke and minding my own business when who should turn up but David Slater, asking me to dance. I said no, but he kept on and Sadie gave me this sort of 'oh, go on' look, so I did. It was a bit tense at first, but when the music got smoochy he got close, and this sudden shock wave went down my back. I didn't expect it at all – I thought those stories about touches driving you mad were just cooked up by old spinsters writing to make a fast buck. It was so strange. I felt all cold and shivery, and when he kissed me I thought I would die. He has certainly been around a bit since the first time we went out together. His kisses have improved!

He walked me home, and we kissed some more. I felt guilty about Jamie, of course, but I couldn't help myself. When he asked if we could get back together I said I'd think about it – after our exams. I couldn't believe I had the strength to say that. But I can't get involved now. It will all be too complicated. Besides, I trusted David Slater once before, didn't I? And I don't want to hurt Jamie.

May 20th

Here we go again. Jenny went out with Sadie and her

boyfriend, Adam, and came back with David Slater! You could have knocked Mike down with a feather. He went to draw the bedroom curtains and saw them snogging away under the lamp-post outside! Jamie is away for the weekend. Mike was furious, and wanted to have it out with Jenny there and then. He thinks she must be sleeping around! I told him I'm sure she's not. She's got more sense – hasn't she?

Catherine left us today – Gloria is back at home, and some kind of community nurse is going in each day to keep an eye on her. When I took Catherine back, Gloria told me she was determined to get her life together this time. She has joined Alcoholics Anonymous, and wants Catherine to join the support group for children of alcoholics. It's wonderful news – it's the first time Gloria has ever properly admitted she has a problem. I just hope she hasn't left it too late.

May 21st

Cathy went home yesterday. We haven't been getting on very well, but I miss her in a funny kind of way. I'm glad her mum wants to stop drinking, but I've read about how hard it is and I'm not hopeful. Poor old Cathy. At least Ted is being good to her. She showed me this lovely gold bangle he bought her last week. Still hasn't left his wife, though . . .

Jamie and I are jogging along as usual. I haven't told him about David, and David is being very co-operative about keeping a low profile for the moment. He will keep phoning me at home, though. Dad gets very upset about it, and says I'm two-timing Jamie. I'm not, though. I'm just trying not to think about anything complicated until after the exams. Only two weeks to the first one. David is working as hard as I am. Next week is half term and then the Fifth Years leave school!!! We only have to come back for the exams. I have signed a little form to say I'm interested to go back for the Sixth Form and take 'A' level English, History and Biology, but that was basically to keep Mum and Dad happy. I haven't decided what I want to do yet.

This year the school is encouraging us to go and get work experience after exams instead of the usual three-week intro. to the Sixth Form. The head says it's because the course 'has been found to be of limited value when compared to the opportunity to broaden the mind provided by work experience'. Dad says it's more to do with saving costs on supply cover for teachers, since they're dropping like flies by the end of the year. It's a bit of a con, I reckon. We don't do the course, but we do take home a ton of reading work to do over the holidays. Still, freedom is freedom. The school are going to help people find work if there's a problem. I'm sure the unemployed across the land would be grateful to know how they intend to do this . . .

May 22nd

I've got a study schedule worked out for next week. I'm going to revise all morning, go out or watch videos or something in the afternoon and then revise again in the evening. Dad has been really good about helping me get the balance of subjects, revision and relaxation right. It's just the sort of thing he has to do at work all the time, he says, and he makes it look so easy he sort of gives me confidence that I can do it.

I've arranged to see Jamie every afternoon next week except one. He has a football match on Thursday, and I'm going round to David's house. I feel like a traitor, but I just can't decide between them without a bit more time.

A parcel of tiny knitted jackets and bonnets arrived this morning, from Gran. They look very cute. Surely our baby won't be that tiny? I'm getting quite excited about the whole thing now. I asked Mum if she would have one of those home births, with everyone standing around watching. She said she wanted every single modern technological doobery going and had no intention of supplying a floorshow for family entertainment! So much for the hippy generation, eh? Dad is going to be at the birth. They're both very into these breathing and floor exercises at the moment. Jon and I fall about the place watching them. All that puffing and panting, at their age! I bet it'll all be wasted anyway. He wasn't there when I was born because I was three weeks early, and Dad was abroad and couldn't get back in time. With Jon he was there all right, but had to leave the room to throw up at the crucial moment ('excitement', he says) and missed the whole thing. He says he's determined not to miss it this time, but we'll see. He'll probably faint. I'm glad I won't be there to be embarrassed by it.

May 25th

Jenny and Jon are not being as supportive of their ageing pregnant mother as they could be. Mike and I are trying to do the homework from the ante-natal classes but whenever we get out the blankets and lie down they howl like hyenas. It's very off-putting. Mike got a splendid tape from a colleague at the office – soothing noises and pulses and animal calls, recorded in the Brazilian rain forests. It is designed to be very relaxing, to take us back to our primeval roots with the earth and the forces of Nature. But we don't get much chance to use it. As soon as we get to the drifting-away-from-consciousness bit, you can bet one of the children will suddenly scream with laughter, or jump out from behind a door pretending to be a warrior or a demented parrot (Jenny's imitation is frighteningly good). I don't think they're taking the birth process very seriously.

Mother sent me some lovely little knitted things for the baby last week. It has inspired me to get out the needles myself. I was very good at knitting as a teenager. I offered to teach Jenny, but knitting is apparently an activity much favoured by dinosaurs and no-one else.

Half term has flown by. Only four days to exams. French comes first. I've spent ages revising for that and for Science, because they feel like the weakest ones. Maths is just about impossible – or was, until Jamie started going through things with me. He's a real wizard at Maths, and makes everything that I couldn't understand at school much clearer. We spent most of our afternoons together showing me how to do bits of Maths I get stuck on. It must have been boring for him but he never complained. That made me feel even worse about being with David on Thursday. We watched daft soap operas on telly, and manhandled one another a lot. It's like we're two different people from the shy, slightly stumbling kids who went out together last year. I thought he was God's gift then. Now I know he's not, but it doesn't matter. It almost makes me fancy him more, to know he has a dark side. Meanwhile, Jamie is practically perfect in every way, like Mary Poppins was. The trouble is, he has about as much sex appeal as she did. I'm really torn between them. I've made it clear to David that I'm still with Jamie, and he says he'll wait – but not for ever.

Half term has flown by for once. I took the week off work so that Jenny did not have to look after Jon. I was worried that the pressure of revision would make things too tense between them for Jenny to get enough done, but she has sailed through the week with the serenity of someone who knows exactly what she wants and where she's going. She had a rigid schedule, which Mike helped her with. To our surprise, she actually stuck to it. She was up by eight, revising, and worked through until lunchtime. Then she went to Jamie's or he came here every afternoon, and at least two of those dates were spent discussing work! At last Jenny seems to have set her sights and decided to work towards good results. I hope she does well: good results at GCSE will set her up for good 'A' levels and make getting a university place so much easier.

In three years' time I could have one child at university and one in playschool!

Well, this is it. Tomorrow my exams start, and there's nothing more I can do. I have worked very hard for the last few weeks, living like a nun sworn to isolation and silence (almost). But I have to admit that I wish now I'd worked harder in the Fourth form. I wasted a lot of time just catching up on notes I didn't take properly last year, and it was time I could have used for revision. Still, it's too late to worry now. I've done the best I could. Mum and Dad say that as long as they know I've done my best, the results won't worry them. But I know if I fail everything they'll be very upset. I'm going to look for a job when the exams are over, just in case. Nothing on this earth would induce me to go back for GCSE retakes. I'm not even sure I want to do 'A' levels. If a good job turns up I probably won't.

Mum has been knitting like something demented for the past few days. The house is being taken over by weird and wonderful garments. Some of them will only fit properly if the baby is born very deformed (the first jacket she knitted had two arms on the same side!). At least it keeps her happy, and while she's busy knitting up little bits of science fiction she's not trying to run my life.

June 3rd

Jenny's exams start tomorrow. I don't think she realizes what a landmark this is in her life. She looked very calm tonight, but perhaps it's all an act. I couldn't sleep a wink before my exams, I remember. So much hinges on good results. The Sixth form won't even let her in if she doesn't get five 'C' passes. I'm sure she will, but I don't look forward to the alternative, which is to go through all this again next year when she retakes them. Mike has been giving her a hand with the stuff she finds hard, and he says her Maths is not bad at all. We're just going to keep fingers and toes crossed.

Jon is fed up with Jenny being the centre of attention at the moment. He is pretending to take exams as well. He sits at the dining room table with all sorts of bits of paper and books, pretending to revise. He wants to be like Jenny so much. Poor little lad – he'll find out soon enough how much fun exams really are.

June 4th

French exam – not as bad as I expected. It's good to start with a reasonable one, for confidence. I'm not sure if I passed, but at least I won't get a really bad grade. It's such a relief to have the exams going on at last. It means the end is in sight.

June 7th

Jenny is not giving any sign about how her exams are going. She seems to be working quite hard on revision. I've only once come home from work to find a friend here – David Slater. Every other day she is poring over her books. She looks a bit pale and washed out. I hope she isn't working too hard. I know the exams are important, but I don't want her to lose all contact with the outside world. I told her that tonight, and she laughed and said thank you, she'd bear it in mind. It's hard when your own child treats you like a fussy old woman.

June 8th

Latin was a real pig of an exam. I don't think 'A' level students should be expected to know half the stuff they were asking. Humanities was a gift from the gods – almost everything I revised showed up in one form or another. Not so Science, unfortunately. The first paper seemed designed to catch me out, and asked all the topics I didn't revise. If the practical and the second paper go like that, I can forget Science. Maths and Art are the next . Art will be a bit of light relief – three hours' drawing will suit me fine. I expect it will be dandelions or dried grasses for the still life, that'll be about all the school can afford! My Art coursework is rather good if I say so myself (and just have) so I'm not too worried.

Although I swore to keep my love life on ice until after the exams it hasn't quite worked out that way. Jamie has been skiving school to spend a bit of time helping me with Maths revision. That was the idea anyway. I didn't ask him to – I'll feel awful if he gets caught – but he's been three times this week. We've done some Maths and then we've spent time just talking or snuggled up on the sofa watching soap opera stuff. Then David found out Jamie was coming round and said he wanted to see me too. That involved a bit of organization. I told Jamie he mustn't skip any more school, and David came round while Mum was at work. We spent very little time studying and lots more time trying to restrain ourselves. I fancy him like mad – but what about Jamie, who's so sweet? And faithful, which I would never again claim for David Slater.

I think the idea of Life after Exams is a myth, put about by those who have a vested interest in keeping teenagers downtrodden and co-operative. The almighty god of the GCSE is totally ruling my life. I can't get away from them wherever I go. All my friends are obsessed with exams – even Jamie, who isn't even taking any this year but wants me to do well. I don't find that sweet any more. It's really getting on my nerves. Why can't he just take me out for a night of fun and passion, instead of droning on about how well I must be doing? David isn't much better. He's desperate to go back to the Sixth Form. He wants to go to University and get an engineering degree. I don't see myself as an engineer's wife, somehow. I'm much more suited to an international banker or foreign diplomat, something like that.

To be frank, I'm fed up with everybody. Even my own family, whom you'd think could be relied on as a port in a storm, can only talk GCSE-speak. Every day I'm interrogated about how it's all going, and each exam is dissected and examined as something of Great National Interest. Jon is the only one who doesn't give a toss. I've tried encouraging him to divert attention from me by indulging in a few boyish pranks, but nothing sends the parents off course. WHEN ARE THESE EXAMS GOING TO END?

It feels as though these blessed exams are ruling our life. Every day we wait with bated breath to hear how Jenny got on with her revision, how well prepared she is for the next exam etc. Over dinner we listen to her account of how the last exam went. There's a long drawn-out post mortem with Mike and me trying to advise or counsel or support or encourage depending on what state Jenny is in. We are all breathing, eating and sleeping exam fever. Jon is being very naughty at the moment because he feels shoved out. Jenny is not being very understanding. She does believe that she and her exams are all that there is to Murray family life. When are these exams going to END?

June 20th

The end is almost in sight – only two more exams to go. The second Science paper was much better than the first, and gave me a bit more confidence for the Practical which was today. My test tube solution was a completely different colour to everyone else's so I'm not too hopeful!

Tomorrow I have English Lit (the Language paper last week was a doddle) and CDT finishes off the torture. My CDT coursework has been hopeless all the way through so I'm not going to break my neck working for the exam. Next week there is also going to be a party – the party to end all parties, apparently – at Cathy's house. Her mum is away (NOT drying out, but a dirty weekend in Somerset, according to Cathy). She goes to Alcoholics Anonymous meetings almost every night, and has met a fellow sufferer who has been on the wagon for years and gives her lots of moral support (that's what Cathy's mum calls it, anyway). It's a real romance, Cathy says, and things are looking up for Cathy and her mum, which is good news. But I digress. While Cathy's mum is away, the mice will play – all night. There'll be about thirty of us, and there's already enough booze stored in various secret places to flow a river! Ted is bringing a few friends to act as bouncers so there'll be no trouble with gate crashers or uncontrollable drunks. It'll be a real rave without the hassle, I think. I can't wait!

Mum has found me a job at her work starting in a couple of weeks. She is thrilled at the idea of working together. I'm not so sure I like that bit, but if I make a good impression they might offer me a permanent job which would solve the problem of having to find something worth leaving school for. I quite fancy the Casualty department – all that blood and gore and drama!

June 20th

I am getting very tired these days. The baby seems to settle in the oddest places, and I keep getting backache. By lunchtime I'm shattered. I'm only doing mornings at Casualty now. Afternoons kill me. I have become quite a fan of one or two afternoon soaps. I sit with my knitting and the television most of the afternoon. I feel my age, particularly at the ante-natal clinic. Most of the other mums-to-be seem to be children themselves. There are only about three of us older parents. We've formed a sort of club, and meet up with each other once a week for mutual encouragement and support. The three babies are all due within a couple of months of each other, so I hope it's a friendship that will last past the births.

I'm going to take my maternity leave from the end of July, which will give me at least six weeks before the baby is due if all goes according to plan. I'm not sure if I'll go back yet; we'll see how it goes. Megan (next door) is quite keen to become a childminder because she's fed up with her job and wants more time at home. That might work out beautifully. But I'm trying not to make too many decisions until after the birth. We don't need my salary any more, with Mike doing so well. I might just stay home and spend more time with the family.

Mavis has suggested I ask Jenny if she wants to work in the Casualty department over the summer. We need someone for filing and liaising with the wards to cover holidays, and if she started before I left she might even be offered something like my job until she starts school again. It's a wonderful opportunity, and Jenny seemed quite enthusiastic. It'll be lovely to work alongside each other.

English Lit wasn't bad at all. Some of the questions were a bit daft, but some of it was even interesting (hard to believe, but true!).

When I got home, Mum was sitting in front of the telly with these two other women she's met at the baby clinic. They're just as old and fat as she is, and they were all sitting there stuffing chocolates and weeping over some really stupid video they'd hired. I pointed out that Mum is always lecturing me about the moral slide of society as evidenced by people who sit around on their backsides doing nothing all day, but she just got snooty and said pregnant women had a duty to their bodies and their 'precious cargo' (that's the way she talks about the baby these days – bring on the sick bucket!) to rest for two hours in the afternoon, and a video was just the right thing to help them relax. Then she sent me off to make a pot of tea while she and her buddies sat in a row in the living room, feet up and bellies bulging like balloons. They looked like roly-poly visitors from another planet.

I had a lovely peaceful day today. I spent the morning baking things for the freezer to tide us over for a few weeks around the birth, and listening to the radio. It's a bit of a pain doing separate vegetarian things for Jenny, but this veggie craze seems to be one of the few permanent resolves in her life. I have to admire her grit. It wasn't easy forsaking bacon sandwiches and roast dinners for bean casserole and soya stew!

In the afternoon Sally and Deborah came over and we watched a film and swapped pregnancy tales and compared notes on how our husbands are likely to measure up. Mike came out middle. Debbie's husband sounds like the original mould for modern man, who can do everything from ironing to cooking a four course dinner and still be in a good mood. Sally's husband sounds hopeless – willing, but not very able. So Mike will do, I suppose. He knows how to change a nappy and he will cook spaghetti bolognese five nights a week if called upon.

Jenny came home in a good mood for once, and made us all some tea. She is shaping up to be a very caring person, and I think she'll get on very well up at the hospital.

June 24th

THAT'S IT! THAT'S IT! THAT'S IT! HALLELUJAH! BRING ON THE DANCING GIRLS ETC. ETC. ETC. EXAMS ARE OVER!

I never want to take another exam as long as I live. Forget 'A' levels and university. I'm going to get a job that pays money and lets you come home at the end of the day with enough time and energy to go out and spend it.

I haven't seen David or Jamie for over a week now, and it's amazing how much more relaxing my life has been as a result. I have thought a lot about the situation I got myself into, and I've come to the conclusion that although I *like* them both, neither one is *quite* what I want. The trouble is, you do actually need to have them both to get one decent boyfriend. Jamie is kind and considerate and very, very sweet but he's a bit of a wimp and not very sexy. David is warm and passionate and makes me feel really weird, but I don't trust him. I need to whip up the courage to end it with both of them, hopefully before Jamie finds out about David because I would never want to hurt him.

I am going to spend tomorrow doing absolutely nothing (except perhaps making a bonfire of my revision notes) and the next day I'll go out shopping for something mega-brill to wear to the party. I have been saving all my money for something really stunning. Neither Jamie nor David is going to be at the party. Jamie isn't invited, which doesn't bother him because he doesn't like Cathy anyway, and David has to go to his cousin's wedding. So I'm going to go a-hunting for a completely new man, and if I find a decent one I'm going to kiss them both goodbye and start afresh.

June 24th

Jenny's exams are over at last. Hallelujah! I gather she and Cathy are going to get together to celebrate next week. Jenny is going to stay the night at Cathy's and they're having a couple of friends round for a 'sleepover'. I'm very happy to see the two girls celebrating together after Cathy has been through so much and been supported by Jenny. I know Gloria will not let things get out of hand. For a start she won't allow alcohol in the house. Her AA programme seems to be doing her so much good, and she has formed a relationship with a lovely man who is himself an alcoholic. They don't like to say they're cured, because they only live one day at a time, but I gather it's over three years since he last took a drink, and that's just the kind of support Gloria needs. I'm really happy for her – and for Catherine and Jenny, whose exams are over, and for the Murray family, which at last can get back to normal.

The party was really good, except that I got a bit drunk. I've never been drunk before, and it doesn't rate as one of my most wonderful experiences. I didn't drink that much, but I may have lost count of the refills. Anyway, I felt fine until the party was almost over. We were all out in the garden – trying to climb a tree, I think, but my memory seems to be a bit hazy – and suddenly I couldn't stand properly. I just made it to the bathroom before I was as sick as anything. Just as well Mum and Dad had agreed to me staying the night – if they had caught me drunk, I would have been skinned alive. If they find out Cathy's mum wasn't actually here last night, it will be bad enough.

This morning I felt awful, as bad as I have ever left in my life. My head is banging so loud I'm surprised no-one else can hear it. I didn't dare tell Mum though. I had to pretend I felt fine, and chat about the party as if nothing was unusual. It was torture.

I don't even like alcohol that much. It wasn't worth it. I'll be more careful next time. I may even go on the wagon, like Cathy's mum.

Apart from that bit, the party was great. The music was good, all my friends were there and no parents hanging around to moan about noise or drink! Best of all I could dance and talk with anybody without any pressure, since David and Jamie were elsewhere. One of the boys in my class, Sam Pattelli, asked me out. He's not bad-looking, and I was on the point of saying yes, when I suddenly realized that one of the best things about the party was being unattached! So I said I was still seeing someone, which is the truth until I can think of a tactful way to dispose of Jamie and/or David. But actually I am toying with the idea of leaving men right out of the picture for a while, and having some fun on my own. Boys make life too complicated.

Sadie was at the party with Adam. She is looking pretty good these days, and she's almost completely better. It was great to see her having so much fun. She and Adam have been going out for ages. I'm glad this romance stuff works for some!

July 3rd

I have a feeling that Jenny got as drunk as a skunk last night. I don't know how it can have happened; I'm sure they must have smuggled it past Gloria, because reformed alcoholics are always the most zealous about such things. When she came back this morning she was exhibiting all the classic signs of hangover. She tried to be very casual, but I've seen that look before too many times to be duped. I bet she was sick, and she hates being sick so I hope it taught her a lesson. Mike and I decided to ignore it, this once. But I hope it's not the beginning of a slide into drunken nights out. She's already boy-mad. In my day it wasn't the done thing to have two boyfriends, but Jenny seems to be aiming for a string of them. Apparently there's a new one on the scene now. Mike thinks it's funny, but I worry about the boys. She starts work with me next week; perhaps she will learn more mature behaviour then.

Jamie and I have finished with each other. There wasn't a row or anything. We were just talking about what we wanted out of life and stuff like that, and he started talking about what would happen to us if I left school for good and he was still there. Suddenly he said he had been wondering lately if we were right for each other. And just as suddenly, we had agreed that we would always be good friends but perhaps that was all there was to us, and we should each look for someone else.

Although we both felt it was the end, I was really crushed when I got home. It feels almost as bad as when David Slater two-timed me, which is stupid because I've been wanting to find a way to end it with Jamie for weeks. I think Jamie understood me better than anyone and being with him was safe and comfortable, like wearing well-washed jeans. David is more exciting, but I don't think we're suited to each other. I can't bring myself to end it, because when I'm with him he makes me feel great. But when we're apart I don't miss him the way I used to, I just get on with life. Maybe I'm destined to live alone always, and men just aren't going to be a part of my life. What a sad thought.

I am getting worried about Mum, and so is Dad. She looks awful, all white and tired and HUGE!! If she's going to do any more growing, we'll have to roll her around, and there's still two months to go. When I look at her it puts me right off having children of my own. I'd never tell her that, of course, but it's true all the same. She also cries at the silliest things. Jon and I are having a very hard time of it. Dad wants her to give up work, but she said the doctor said she would be OK until the end of July. I don't think she's telling the truth. One look at her is enough for anyone to tell she is not OK.

Dad and I have decided to do as much as we can about the house to try and keep Mum off her feet. Jon is being a little brat, of course. At first he said he wanted jobs to do, too. So we gave him setting and clearing the table, and cleaning the bathroom. But he doesn't fancy those chores. He wants to be in charge of washing the car and mending things that go wrong – very useful, to have a seven-year-old handyman! Now he just sulks a lot and pesters Mum. I'm trying to be understanding because I know it's hard for him to have everyone so preoccupied, but if he wants to celebrate his eighth birthday he'd better shape up.

July 8th

Jenny and Jamie are not going out any more. I think Jamie must have been the one who called it off, because Jenny is looking like a cat with a cold. She's also a bit snappy. She doesn't want to talk though – when Mike asked whether Jamie was coming round at the weekend, she just said, 'We're not an item any more.' Mike made a joke about more fish in the sea, and at least one of them was already in her net (meaning David Slater) but it didn't go down too well.

The weather has been very hot for the last few days, which makes me even more tired. I could sleep for ever. By the time Jon gets home from school I feel completely exhausted. The doctor at the ante-natal clinic thinks I should give up work immediately so that I can rest more, but it's only part-time and I did promise I would work to the end of July. They are so short-staffed with holidays etc. already. I'm going to have to find ways of taking things easier. Mike talked to Jenny last night and they've worked out a few ways to help. Jenny is going to cook the dinner twice a week, and so's Mike. This should be an experience and a half!

First day at work, in the Casualty department. I had a great time. Everyone was really nice to me and showed me what to do and so on. Everyone knew who my mum was, which was highly embarrassing. Mum keeps trying to show me off like some kind of ornament. It would be bad enough at the best of times to have to admit to kinship, but how do you think it feels to be sixteen and have a pregnant – VERY pregnant – mother? The jokes about built-in babysitters, and how my children will have an aunty or uncle much the same age, got on my nerves after the five hundredth time.

Apart from that, I enjoyed the work. I was mostly doing filing and filling out record cards, but I did get to visit a couple of wards. The hospital seems a nice place to work, with everyone so friendly. The doctors and nurses look very busy. I saw a group of them in the canteen at lunchtime and tried to imagine myself like that, wearing a uniform and holding life and death in my hands. They looked so at ease with who they were, and looked like they were having a real laugh. I suppose it's one profession where most people you work with are the same age as you, which would be fun. But I'm only a lowly clerical assistant, and mustn't get ideas above my station. At least with my job you don't have to study all the time. I think I could hack it here in Casualty, if they gave me a job. I haven't said that to Mum and Dad, of course . . .

Jenny started work with me today. She was quite a success, and I was proud of her. She looked so calm, so mature when she was being told what to do. Mavis said how lucky I was to have such a sensible, cheerful daughter. I've never thought of Jenny like that! At home she is moody and singularly lacking in sense sometimes. But watching her go about her business I realized just how well she has turned out. It is lovely being able to work together. Jenny seemed to appreciate having me there to ease her in and introduce her to everybody, and I'm sure that helped her first day to go so well.

July 13th

At my ante-natal appointment, Dr Brown was insistent that I give up work. She asked if I really felt letting colleagues down at work was worth risking my own health — and the baby's. That did it, of course. I felt stupid. Of course the baby comes first. I called Mavis and the manager, and they both said they understood and told me off for not giving up earlier. I still feel a bit guilty, as though I've left them in the lurch. And I feel a bit sad for Jenny, too, who thought I would be there with her for at least another couple of weeks. But mostly I feel relieved. I do need the rest. I think this baby is going to be a big, hefty footballer.

Mum has given up work. At last that daft doctor noticed how bad she's looking and advised her to stay home. It's about time. Now I don't have to worry about her collapsing at work and me not knowing what to do (although I suppose there's no better place to collapse than a Casualty department). Another good thing is that I am working on my own now. No offence to Mum, but it was really mega-embarrassing having her hovering at my shoulder all the time.

The Casualty charge-nurse told me today that I'm doing really well and they're all glad to have me on board. That made me feel great.

After lunch I had to take some files up to the geriatric ward. The temperature outside must have reached the eighties today, but the old people were still sitting there with dressing gowns on – and the radiators were warm, too. I could hardly breathe it was so stuffy. I felt so sorry for some of them. They were just staring into space, or watching the visitors who gathered around other people's beds. It churned me up to see one old lady looking so wistfully at the next bed, where there were flowers and chocs and visitors. Her bedside cabinet was empty, except for one card. I stopped to chat for a couple of minutes, and her face sort of lit up. I'm going to try and go back every day before I leave work. It's such a little thing for me, and such a big thing for her.

I had a blazing row with David today, and that's that. He's been away for ten days, on holiday with his family. I had forgotten he was back today (not like the old days, when every moment away from him was counted and grieved over!) and I arranged to go round to Sadie's. Adam's away too and she's really missing him, so I said

I'd keep her company. Then David shows up on the doorstep expecting me to drop everything and go out with him. I told him I'd arranged to see Sadie and he more or less demanded that I tell her I couldn't go! Well, I wasn't having that. It was a genuine mistake that I forgot today was the day he got back from France and we hadn't fixed anything. Anyway I don't see why that should automatically mean we have to be together every spare moment. I said I'd see him tomorrow, but he got sulky and sort of made a situation where I felt I had to choose between him and Sadie. No contest. Suddenly I remembered all the hurt he had put me and Sadie through in the past, and the row got out of hand. I said a few things I shouldn't have, and a few things I should have said a long time ago and didn't have the nerve for, and he said, 'If that's the way you feel, maybe we should just call it a day,' and I said, 'Fine.' Then he stomped off. Maybe he'll be back, maybe not. I don't know which I would prefer.

Sadie and I drowned our sorrows with cider and loads and loads of cheese and onion crisps (these are denied to us when we're out with the boys, because of the smelly breath). And we had a good time!

July 15th

Jenny got her come-uppance today, for playing both ends against the middle. She and David had a row, and now it appears to be over between them. I know she needs to be taught a lesson about faithfulness and loyalty – she was basically doing to David and Jamie what David had done to her – but I do feel a bit sorry for her. She should be going out and having fun at her age, and instead she's lost both boyfriends and has to spend her time watching TV at Sadie's house. I don't know why I'm complaining – I'd rather she was there than at some night-club. But it feels like a shame, nonetheless.

96

I feel a lot better for having given up work. I sit around a lot and dream of babies. I only think of the nice things. I've forgotten about the sleepless nights and the mound of nappies and the constant crying. At least I've tried to.

Mike and Jenny have lived up to their word and have more or less taken charge of the house. Even Jon does his bit and lays the table and washes up. I keep a napkin handy to wipe the smudges off the cutlery before I eat. The food is pretty basic if Mike cooks, but edible. When it's Jenny's turn we all have to eat ambitious vegetarian casseroles, because she can't cope with two things cooking at once and yet scorns anything simple. Jon pulls disgusted faces and has fish fingers afterwards. Jenny puts his feelings down to immaturity, and doesn't take it personally. I wish I was seven years old and didn't have to worry about tact and diplomacy. But I appreciate the effort, and do my best. When she goes out, or to bed, I raid the freezer!

I hate to say it, but Dad is right. He said this job would get to me in the end, and it has. At first it was very interesting, but now I'm quite bored and the thought of another three weeks is mind-blowing. By rights, I ought to be on holiday somewhere. We're not going away as a family because of the baby. Dad says we'll have a longer holiday abroad next year to make up for it, but I'll be seventeen then and family holidays aren't likely to be my style.

It's hard to get up early in the morning and use the whole day for shuffling paper and filling in forms. I enjoy chatting to the patients – I go up to the geriatric ward every day if I can, and watching the nurses at work has made me think seriously about going back to school and getting 'A' levels at least. I still have no idea what I want to do, but the idea of going out into the world if I can get a job is fading. I might consider nursing or physiotherapy – something that helps people but has a bit of a challenge to it as well. One thing I definitely know is that office work is not for me. I'm not organised enough, and I need more going on. Today they asked me to go on the reception desk for an hour. That's another thing. I thought it would be just like the telly – desperately ill bodies wheeling through on trollies for a fight to save the last dying gasp. But most of the time it's sprains, cuts and fractures. Most of our patients manage to sit around for a couple of hours waiting to be seen without collapsing on the floor or having violent confrontations with estranged relatives. Maybe it's more exciting at night, but I'm too young to do the night shift. So here I am, earning money but too tired to spend it. I had a bit of a moan to Dad and he grinned and said, 'Welcome to Independence!' Not very sympathetic:

Maybe I've just got used to seeing her like this, but Mum looks positively beautiful at the moment. She's a bit far away and day-dreamy – planning for the baby, I expect – and it's like she's living in another dimension to the rest of the family. She looks like a great, calm Mother Earth. I'm really looking forward to seeing the baby. I can't wait to see what it is, what it looks like. When I'm twenty-six and have a place of my own she or he will be ten. If it's a girl, maybe she'll come and stay with me sometimes while Mum and Dad go away together. (If it's a boy, it'll be another Jon – no thanks!) Jon wants a boy but not very strongly. He's just keen to be the big brother for a change. For me, a girl would be much, much nicer. She would look up to me, and I could teach her loads of things. I wish I had spent more time with Jon when he was tiny. He always seemed to be such a pain, but I could have been a better big sister to him. Still, it's not too late. I'll be able to sharpen up my skills on two children soon.

August 6th

I wish this baby would hurry up. I would be more than happy for it to arrive four weeks early. I'm hot, uncomfortable and miserable. Jon gets on my nerves all the time, Mike and Jenny most of the time. Above all, I get on my own nerves. I feel like a whale, a mound of blubber. I can't bend down to do the gardening, the heat makes me feel terrible and I wish Mike and I had never been to Paris. I must have been mad to want another baby. In ten years my life would have been my own again and now I'm back to square one. I could scream, but it wouldn't do any good. No-one else in the family would hear me.

I was moaning on to Sadie about being bored and done out of a holiday today, and she came up with a great idea. Her aunty has a caravan near the seaside in Sussex, a place called Littlehampton. Sadie phoned and asked if we could stay there for a few days and she said yes! We thought we'd ask Cathy as well. It'll be a laugh, just the three of us with no men. We were good mates before boyfriends came on the scene. Life was so uncomplicated. I thought I might have a bit of trouble with the parents, but surprise surprise, they said OK. The caravan is on a small private site and Mum said it sounded very nice. Little does she know that we don't plan to be doing much on the site except sleeping.

I don't feel quite as miserable as I did when I last wrote, but I'm still anxious to get this thing over and done with. Jenny is going away for a few days soon, down to Sadie's aunt's caravan in Sussex, near Brighton. Sadie's mother phoned me before Jenny even asked if she could go, to tell me they were hatching this plan. She reassured me about the site, which is a quiet little one, and also there are good friends of the family staying there for the whole Summer who'll keep a quiet eye on the girls for us. So when Jenny told us about it we said yes. Her face was a picture. She had her arguments all lined up ready; she was almost disappointed she didn't have to fight us. She doesn't know there'll be people watching over them. It's a good way to learn a bit of independence. Meanwhile, she's being very sweet to say thank you to us for letting her go.

My life is getting better and better! Not only do I have a great holiday planned with my friends and no parents in sight, but there's a gorgeous (no, GORGEOUS – only capitals will do) student nurse on the Casualty department. His name's George, he's nearly nineteen and he's got it all. He's tall, great-looking, with a sense of humour and the loveliest brown eyes I've seen anywhere. When I told Sadie about him she fell about laughing. All right, Nurse George sounds weird, but only to the sexist minds of the ignorant. George is a bit of an old-fashioned name, but his mum's West Indian and it's no big deal over there. He goes to Jamaica every year for his holidays, to stay with his gran. Makes Littlehampton sound a bit dull, dunnit? Never mind.

Sadie reminded me that I'd given up men. That was an unfair and low comment. True, I enjoyed the single life for a while, but to waste George on any lesser female would be nothing short of a crime. I think he fancies me, but he hasn't asked me out. Yet. There's still time, though . . .

I know that look in my daughter's eye. There's a new man on the scene. Someone at work, must be – she's never been so keen to get up and get out in the mornings. I called Mavis last night and asked her who it was. She thinks it's the new first year student, George. Mavis says he's a nice enough lad. He's certainly put a sparkle in Jenny's eye.

Only three and a half weeks to go. Come on baby, get a move on.

I'm beginning to wonder if there's something seriously wrong with George. I've done everything a girl can do without wearing a sign round her neck begging for attention, but he's either impervious to my charms or he's too shy to exist in this world. He smiles, he talks to me, he asks me about my social life and my friends and what I like doing (I've invented half a dozen extra things in case I hit something he's really keen on, to no avail) but he never gets round to that crucial question. Mavis told me today that he asked her if I had a boyfriend. She had said 'No-one serious'. I could have died. It makes me look as though I play the field and never get serious. I asked her to put him right on that one. I have no boyfriend at all, and am looking for someone sensible and kind and committed, I said. Mavis laughed and said she got the picture. It was so embarrassing, but necessary. Honestly, the degradation you have to go through to get your man!

Whatever Mavis said to George, it didn't work. He is just the same as before – no date. I'm going to have to give up soon. I leave in three days' time, and then Sadie and Cathy and I are off to Sussex. So, who cares? Plenty more fish in the sea, as Dad is so fond of saying. He's got a couple more chances, and then it's his loss.

Mavis came round to see me yesterday. She brought some lovely flowers and cheered me up no end with her account of what's going on at work. Our Jenny and George are providing quite a bit of entertainment for the whole department. He drools over her from afar, I under-

stand, but can't quite bring himself to make a move. Instead, he tries to make sure he ends up in the same place as her, or the same lift. The charge nurse told him off yesterday for daydreaming as Jenny walked past, and he blushed like mad when she smiled sympathetically at him. Mavis says you have to admire Jenny's patience. She's making it as easy as possible for poor George to make his move and Mavis says it's like watching a walking 'Get Your Man' video. Jenny has tried every trick Mavis knew about and a few new ones she wished she'd learned when she was Jenny's age! Oh, to be a teenager again? Not likely! Mind you, I thought these days it was all equal rights. So why doesn't Jenny ask George out? I must ask her tomorrow.

My last day at work. The staff bought me a box of chocs and said thanks for all my work. Mrs Drew, the old lady I've been visiting up on the geri ward was quite upset to hear I'm leaving. I've promised to send her a postcard from Sussex and to see her as soon as I get back. She has no-one, poor old thing. Her daughter and son-in-law live only twenty miles away, and they've only visited her once. She could go home soon if there was someone to look after her, but they won't. The hospital Social Worker is sorting out home helps and stuff but it won't be the same as having a loving family round you. I hope I'm not like that when Mum and Dad are old. I'd like to think that however trying they were, I'd still be there for them. Dad says there are two sides to every story and I shouldn't judge, but it's hard not to. I think I might like to nurse old people, when I'm trained.

But enough of work. It's time for play. We're off tomorrow! As for George, well, I've given him up as a hopeless cause. You can stretch a woman's patience too far! I said goodbye and kissed him on the cheek. He said he'd miss me and I said I'd miss him too, and then I left. So much for my dreams!

Talking of dreams, I don't suppose I'll be having very nice ones tonight. My results are due tomorrow, or the day after at the latest. My whole future could be in the balance here, not to mention the balance of peace and quiet in this house. If I've done really badly Mum and Dad are going to start talking retakes and More Effort and Less Socializing and other horror stories.

Well, results did indeed arrive. Here they are in all their glory: English Lang and Humanities, A(!), Art, B; French, English Lit, Science and Maths, C; Latin and

CDT, D. So I did OK. I didn't expect to get Latin and didn't work too hard for CDT, so that's fair. But towards the end I was flogging myself to death over Maths and Science. If I'd put more effort into coursework I would have done better. Ah well. Mum and Dad were pleased, and didn't mind about the 'D's. I think Mum half-expected me to fail everything. She's never really believed I've worked hard, but I have. I expect I will go back to school – I can get a better job with 'A' levels, or get into nursing training more easily.

Sadie and Cathy and I met round at Sadie's. Cathy got 'D's and 'E's in everything except Maths (C) and she's going to have to do the retake course. Sadie got 'B's and 'C's except for 'A' in Science. After all that worry about missed school, she did better than any of us. I'm pleased for her, of course. We're saving the real celebrations (and consolations, in Cathy's case) for tomorrow, when we are on our first independent trip into the real, parentless world!

August 26th

Jenny got her GCSE results today. She did very well, and only got a poor grade in CDT and Latin. Naturally we were hoping for nine straight 'A's, but two will do! The most important thing is that she can go back to the Sixth Form and doesn't need to take any exams again, so she can do the full three 'A' level course ready for university.

We are all very proud of her. Even Jon made her a 'well done' card, and my mother is going to send her some money to spend on a celebration. I'll leave that as a surprise for when she's back from holiday. She'll be broke then. It's very strange watching her get ready for a holiday on her own. I hope she'll be all right. I'm glad Sadie's relatives are there to keep an eye.

Well, it's not quite city life, but it's good enough. The caravan is quite large and has its own little garden around it, complete with picket fence. There are only about thirty caravans on the whole site, so there's no clubhouse or disco or takeaway or anything. But it is quite near the beach and there's a funfair and loads of cafes etc. at the seafront. We can get a bus from here into Brighton, too. We did that last night and it was good fun with all the lights etc. But Cathy met a man – surprise surprise – and suddenly announced she wouldn't be coming back with us. We tried to persuade her to come back on the bus, but Cathy was never one to do the decent or the sensible thing, so we came back without her and sat playing cards, worried to death, until two this morning when she finally had the grace to return. She seemed genuinely surprised that we had waited up, and even more surprised that we were worried about her. She was nearly legless and there was a bit of a row, but she said sorry and we agreed it wouldn't happen again. All the same, things were a bit strained today.

Cathy announced that she had a date this afternoon with the man she met the other night. I asked her what Ted would think – they're supposedly still a couple and she just shrugged and said he wasn't going to know, was he? There was another row. I wanted to tell Dad but how could I? He'd simply drive down here and collect us all, like little schoolkids. Cathy is nearly seventeen (going on thirty-five, by experience) and she should know what she's doing. At least this one is nearer her own age – he's only twenty, and Ted is seven years older. We made her promise she wouldn't do anything daft and she'd be back by midnight. I told her we'd call the police if she wasn't back, and I think she could see I meant it.

I wanted to go out to the funfair but Sadie was too tired. She still feels the effects of the operations she had a bit, I think. She was also worried about Cathy and thought we ought to stay in until she got back. So we played cards again.

August 30th

The last couple of days have been quiet, but nice. We have spent most of the day lounging on the beach and the evenings roaming around. The countryside is very pretty. Cathy has been a bit quiet since her date the other night (she came back early, about ten o'clock) but she won't talk about it. She didn't arrange to see him again, so I guess something went wrong. Perhaps she's missing Ted. Sadie has been a bit quiet too, but I think it's because she's still tired all the time. We certainly haven't seen any night life – apart from having dinner with a family two caravans down who turned out to be friends of Sadie's aunty and her mum. They fed us and let us watch 'Coronation Street' on their telly. We certainly do live in exciting times. Tomorrow we go home – Dad's coming to pick us up, and he's bringing Jon down for the day. I have missed them all, in a funny sort of way. I felt a bit funny being away from Mum, which was odd. I suppose it's because she's pregnant and deep down I'm worried the baby will come early and I'll miss it. Anyway, it'll be good to be home.

It's good to be home. Mum looks even bigger, though I know that can't be possible. I am looking forward to this baby so much.

There were a couple of bits of mail waiting for me. Jamie sent me a postcard from Spain, and Gran sent me some money for my holiday (typical Gran timing!). Best of all, George sent a little note asking if I'd call him if I wanted to go to his sister's wedding with him next week! No prizes for guessing my answer to that one! As long as the baby doesn't choose that very day to come, just try and keep me away!

Jenny and her friends came home today. They all look very tanned and relaxed, and apparently had a good time. Our spies on the camp told Sadie's mother that their behaviour was exemplary and they were well tucked up in bed by eleven every night with no sign of riotous living. They clearly had a good time just relaxing on the beach and talking far into the night, as girls do at that age.

I have missed Jenny. Her being away has made me realize how much more mature she is nowadays. It used to be a bit of a strain having her around, to be honest. But now I can see that she has become someone I rely on, and she's even quite a good big sister to Jon. I hope the new baby will enjoy having such a grown-up sister, and will win Jenny round to thinking that a new baby is not such a bad idea after all. It's not going to be long before we all find out!

The holidays are over and I'm almost beginning to wish I had decided to get a job. The amount of reading I have to do before term starts is horrific. We were supposed to make a start at the end of last term and 'pace ourselves' (Potter-speak) over the holidays. But there was always something better to do . . . I started reading 'Mill on the Floss' but it's so boring I can hardly keep my eyes open. Trust our school to choose the old-fashioned 'A' level syllabus. Someone told me that there are some schools doing really modern books. We've got Chaucer, Shakespeare, George Eliot, Milton and Yeats. I am not going to try and think of how this might be useful to society in the twentieth century, I'm just going to get on with it. History looks more interesting. We get to go on field trips and study old documents etc. I chose Biology because it will be useful if I do decide to go into nursing, and because it was the one part of Science I understood, but I'm not expecting to enjoy it.

All in all it looks like hard slog – again. But at least we'll be treated with a bit more respect by the teachers, and we have our own common room and stuff, and a bit more freedom. As Mum says, two years isn't much when you look at it in relation to a whole lifetime. I'll survive.

I phoned George to tell him I could go to the wedding with him. He stuttered and stumbled a bit but sounded very pleased, which was sweet. I don't have to go to the official bit, just the evening party. He's going to meet me after work tomorrow, to fill me in on the family. Just an excuse of course, but who's complaining?

1st September

Jenny has finally found her niche at last. No sooner had she unpacked and sorted herself out from the holiday than she was getting stuck in to some preparatory work for her Sixth Form. I bet she can't wait to get absorbed in some real literature after that modern pap they did for GCSE. I look forward to long chats about our great heritage of English Literature. I expect she will be able to teach me a thing or two before she's done.

I had lunch with Liz today. Her Simon is still insisting he won't go back to school. He wants to work at the local garden centre. Liz really wants him to go to unversity but he claims it's a waste of time because he wants to be free and easy and earn money NOW. I half-expected Jenny to go and look for a job, but she set her sights on 'A' levels right from the start and never wavered. I have to admire her dedication.

I phoned round all my friends to find out how they did: no-one had a real disaster except Natalie Warren, who only got 'C' in Maths and French. The rest were 'E's and 'F's. Mind you, she did have to fit studying and revising around the most hectic social life known on this planet, so she can't be very surprised. Sadie says her mum hit the roof and if Natalie doesn't go back and do the Fifth Form again her life won't be worth living. Thank God I was spared that. David Slater got all 'B's except for English (C) and Science (A). Clever clogs. He will be in my Biology set which might be a bit of a strain. But Sadie and I are going to be doing History and English together, which will be great.

Mum thinks the baby will be early. She says it could come at any moment, so everyone is going round on tenterhooks waiting for her first groan. She says it's not like that, and it's only on telly that women suddenly clutch themselves and start to drop the sproglet right there on the spot, but I'm going to be ready for anything. After all, having two babies doesn't make you an expert on all eventualities, does it?

Dad is looking like a schoolboy waiting for an all-important football match. There is a look of grim determination and earnestness in his approach to things these days. He leaves a great list of phone numbers before he leaves in the morning so that Mum can contact him. If he's out and about, his secretary phones Mum at least twice a day for an update. She must be sick and tired of all the fuss, so I'm trying to give her a bit of space.

I met George outside the pub for a drink after he had finished at the hospital. He doesn't drink alcohol at all, hardly. He says it's because he's seen too many people wheeled into Casualty after drunken brawls. So he drinks low or no alcohol drinks. That's my kind of man: we sipped Coke together and talked, then he saw me to

112

the top of my road. (I don't want Mum teasing me yet. I haven't told her it's George I fancy. As soon as she knows, she'll be gossiping with Mavis.) I don't want to cheapen the experience by writing vulgar words from romantic novels, so I'll just write that George is the best yet, from all angles. He is from a completely different planet to Nick, David or Jamie.

4th September

I dreamed about the baby last night. It was a little boy, with lots of blond hair and big blue eyes, and he was smiling up at me. It was so real that when I woke up I reached out for him, and was surprised to find him not there. It was so strange. Maybe the baby is sending me a message, saying get ready now. I have felt for some days that he will be early; I half-expected him last week. But now I'm sure it won't be long.

Mike and Jon are being wonderful, so caring and concerned. Mike makes sure I know where he is twenty-four hours a day, and Jon won't go to friends for tea in case he's not here when the time comes. Only Jenny seems a bit aloof. I thought she had come round to the idea of the baby, and she says she is looking forward to it. But she isn't taking much interest. She went off very mysteriously yesterday to meet 'a friend' and came back all gooey and misty-eyed. I asked if she had a good time and she sighed and simpered, 'oh, yes' with an expression that could only be properly described by one of those Mills and Boon novelists. She's not saying who it is, but I reckon it has to be George from Casualty. I shall get all the details from Mavis soon. No doubt if it lasts longer than a couple of dates we'll be allowed a privileged glimpse of the latest poor lamb.

There's something very wrong with Cathy. I phoned her to make arrangements to meet up and go to school together for our first day back, and she sounded really funny. She's decided she may not go back after all! This is all very sudden. She was going to do 'A' level Maths and some retakes; she was sounding quite keen to get going once we had our results and she went in to school to see the Head of Sixth. Now she wants to do something different, but she doesn't know what. It sounded fishy to me, so I asked what was really up. I thought it must be her mother – again. But she said no. Then Cathy, who is as tough as old boots, actually started to cry! It must be bad. I persuaded her to come round tomorrow, before I go to the wedding party, and I'll drag it out of her if necessary. Meanwhile, it's three a.m. and I can't sleep. What with Mum about to give birth literally any minute and Cathy all in pieces, I'm not very calm myself.

9th September

Well, this is the day the baby was due, and I'm still here. The children are back at school, and I spent the day sitting in an armchair, basically, and waiting. I had about six calls, including one from Jenny and two from Mike, asking if I was still here. It got very annoying. I saw the doctor briefly and she said all looked well, we'll just have to wait. I can't believe it's going to be late. I was so sure. The day dragged on and on, and Jon was a real pest. He knew the due date and can't understand why the hospital don't just produce the baby on the day they promised. He sounds like a disgruntled housewife whose carpet hasn't arrived! Maybe he thinks childbirth is a bit like cooking a packaged meal in a microwave. I thought Mike had explained the process to him, but obviously I should have done it myself. I haven't the energy now, so I keep fobbing him off and telling him to be patient. I wish I could be patient. Come on, Baby!

10th September

I haven't had the heart to write a diary entry for the last few days. It's been awful, just awful. Cathy came round the day after I phoned her and it all spilled out. She got 'a bit drunk' (for which, read legless) when she was with that bloke she met down in Sussex and they got carried away. Now she thinks she's pregnant! And she's not even sure if it would be Ted's or this other man's. I couldn't believe she could be so stupid. Hasn't she listened to any of that stuff they've told us at school about AIDS? Not to mention the stupidity of risking pregnancy when there are so many contraceptives on the market she could drown in them if she wanted to.

I was surprised how angry I felt – sympathy for the poor little baby who was going to get mixed up in this mess, mostly. But I knew it wouldn't help to show the anger, so I tried to stay calm and just listen and get the facts right. Cathy's period was due five days ago and she's usually like clockwork. It doesn't look good. She hasn't had the guts to go to a doctor and she spent all her money on holiday, so she can't buy one of those DIY pregnancy tests either. She cried and cried, and kept saying she was sorry to drag me into it. She doesn't want an abortion but she doesn't want a baby either and she's scared of anybody knowing. She said she would have told my mum but she can't with Mum being pregnant herself. I agree it's too much to put on Mum's plate just at the moment. I wish she would hurry up and have this baby and get back to normal.

Anyway, we took a bus into town and I gave Cathy the money for a pregnancy test. Then we went back to my house and locked ourselves in my room. Cathy was

115

shaking so much she couldn't even read the instructions. I had to tell her what to do. Off she went to the bathroom, and came back with the test tube. Negative. But the instructions say you need to do a second test five days later, just to be sure. So that's another wait. Frankly, she's in such a state that I can't be sure she did the test properly. I didn't feel I could go in the bathroom with her and supervise her peeing, but maybe I should have! We've got to go through all this again in five days. I can't bear it.

My date with George should have been great, but this spoiled it. I was so worried I couldn't have as good a time as I usually would. George's family are amazing. There are about fifty thousand of them, and they're all extroverts – dancing, singing, laughing. They treated me as if they'd known me for years. How come George is so shy? It's one of those eternal mysteries I'll have to ask him about one day. I told him about Cathy – not her name, just the circumstances so he'd know I wasn't going off him, just couldn't relax properly. He said I was a really true friend, and he hoped it all worked out. We kissed – very gentle and quite long kisses, until his mother saw us and screamed with laughter. She called George's sisters over and they made jokes about him being a real goer and a fast worker. Actually, thinking about it maybe I *can* understand why George is so uptight . . .

Cathy is in the clear; her period started this morning. The whoops of joy could be heard clear across the playground outside the girls' loo and we were looked at VERY suspiciously when we emerged. But we didn't care. It must have been all the tension that stopped things happening, waiting for results and then realizing what she'd done with this lad in Sussex. But I think – so she says, anyway – that it's taught Cathy a lesson. She's not going to tell Ted, because they're getting genuinely serious. I think that's a mistake. There shouldn't be secrets if you really love someone, and besides if this man is as casual about sex with everyone as he was with Cathy, then I think Ted has a right to know about the risk Cathy took. But I think she'll see that in the end, and I couldn't come the heavy with her when I looked at the sheer relief and joy on her face today.

Mum is still with us. We try to jolly her along with little jokes about it, but I can see she's tired of waiting. Who wouldn't be!

12th September

I'm still here. 'Still here, then?' If anybody says that to me once more I think I might have to do them serious bodily harm. The woman in the corner shop, the lollipop man at Jon's school, the milkman, my friends – some of whom should know better – and my own family think it's terribly witty. 'Still here, are we?' Ho rotten ho. If this baby doesn't come soon I am going to forget about giving it a reasonable name. It may well end up being called Theophilus or Percibald. That will teach it to keep me waiting.

Sitting around like a beached whale does give me the opportunity to observe life in detail, however, and I have noticed that Jenny is behaving in a very peculiar fashion.

117

She and Cathy have been thick as thieves the last few days. They go around looking like prophets of doom. I suppose Cathy's boyfriend must have dumped her and Jenny is propping her up. I hope Cathy hasn't involved her in anything too heavy. If Gloria has fallen off the wagon again it may well be the last time. Her health is precarious enough as a result of past drinking spells, without adding to it. Poor Cathy. What a life. I hope when she eventually has a family of her own it works out better for her than what she was brought up with.

I spent ALL weekend doing assignments, and George spent all weekend studying for his exams in October. We had about two hours together on Saturday night, and we were both too washed out to do anything except go to the pub and watch a darts match. I felt like a Darby and Joan old couple. We've promised ourselves a real treat when George's exams are over. We're going to go to the theatre and have a meal as well – a real night on the town. Poor old George has been saving for it. I was really touched when he told me. He gets a pittance for all the work he does. I insisted that we use my money for at least half the costs. I still have a bit tucked away from working at the hospital and babysitting, and Mum has been paying me for doing extra housework and Jon-minding. In fact, I'm quite a wealthy woman, and what better use for a modern woman's money than support-ing the man she loves? Well, maybe love is a bit strong, but George is definitely up there with a chance!

14th September

I'm still here.

15th September

I'm still here. I've had backache all day and should have rested, but for some reason found myself defrosting the freezer instead, which didn't help the backache. But I'm still here, all right.

This has been the biggest day of my life so far, and it's only ten o'clock. Bigger than being five, or sixteen, or going to secondary school. Bigger than my first date, or even seeing Jon after he was born, because I was too young to really understand it. But early this morning, at eleven minutes past seven, my new baby sister was born. Elizabeth Joanna Murray weighed seven pounds and three ounces, and she and Mum are fine.

Dad woke me up just after two o'clock this morning to tell me that he was taking Mum to the hospital. I watched them go, with Mum in her nightie and overcoat and Dad carrying her bag, and I felt like their mother seeing them off for the first day of school: proud, nervous, excited and a bit scared. We didn't wake Jon. I sat in the living room watching old videos, trying not to think about what could go wrong. The telephone woke Jon just before eight o'clock. It was Dad, telling us about Elizabeth and to get a taxi right away. He met us just outside the hospital and took us to Mum.

Elizabeth is the most exquisite little doll. I can't describe her without tears filling my eyes. I expected her to be red and wrinkled, but she's like porcelain. She has a dusting of dark hair and enormous dark blue eyes which stare out at the world as if she can't quite make sense of the lunatics who are looking down on her. Oh Elizabeth, you'll learn all about us lunatics in time.

Jon was transfixed. He just kept staring and staring and when Dad wedged him into a chair and gave him the baby to hold you could see he was literally holding his breath. He was so sweet. I held her too, and it pulled at me to see her staring up into my face. She waved a little hand at me as if she was saying hello. She has long, graceful fingers. It is such a responsibility, being a big sister. I never felt it so much with Jon.

Jon is desperate to get to school to tell his teachers

and friends about the baby. We've just come home to get some breakfast, and then I'll take him in and explain. Then there's a lot of housework to be done to get ready for the baby coming home. They hope to be here later today, if Mum and Elizabeth are passed as fit by the doctor. But I had to write down how I felt, in case I forget that first moment I saw her in all the rush and hurry that will follow us now.

18th September

It is three a.m. and I am snatching a few quiet moments to record here what I've been waiting to record for nearly nine months. On September 16th at 7.11 a.m. Elizabeth Joanna Murray joined the world, whole and perfect and beautiful. Mike and I cannot believe our luck. Three healthy children is a gift almost too precious to comprehend.

Lizzie is a contented, beautiful little creature. She has not cried half as much as the other two did, and she has already wrapped all four of us round her little finger. She is sleeping peacefully now, full of milk and kisses. Long may it last, this eat and sleep stage. She trusts me completely: no arguments, no fuss. I have one daughter at the beginning of her childhood and another daughter about to leave childhood and become an adult, and my little son is in between. I hope we will always be as happy and harmonious as we have been in these couple of days since Lizzie's birth.

I'm waiting for something bad to happen, because I have a sneaking feeling no-one can be this happy for ever. But every day just gets better and better. Elizabeth is fantastic; the novelty hasn't worn off yet. We call her 'Little Lizzie' and she's definitely the boss around here, but we don't mind. Jon and I have made such plans to take her out places when she's old enough to toddle off with us. Mum and Dad are happier than I've seen them for a long time – but very, very tired! They are so laid back I could probably plan to hitch-hike singlehanded around the world and they wouldn't turn a hair.

Jon and I are doing our best to muck in. The funny thing is, neither one of us feels jealous, or shoved out. The family seems almost to have been waiting for Lizzie, and now she's here it seems the most natural thing in the world. So home is great, and my friends are happy – Cathy and Ted are going to get engaged, she says, although she still hasn't told him about Brighton and he still hasn't left his wife, so it's a funny kind of engagement – and Sadie and Adam are jogging along. George and I are a good match, too. We are attracted to each other but we're also really good friends, and that's just what I need right now.

In fact the only blot on my horizon is the first English essay, which is due in tomorrow. It's an in-depth study of one of the main characters from 'Mill on the Floss'. I have a feeling it won't be ready, since I haven't actually read the book yet! I'm going to be in trouble (what else is new?).

But then, who said a girl can have everything?

Adjust your Mobile? Change your Nappy? A little more Drinky?
My New Boss....